A Candlelight Ecstasy Romance®

"DO YOU REALLY MEAN TO STAY FOR SIX MONTHS?" SHE ASKED, HOPING THAT HE'D SAY HE'D BE GONE IN TWO WEEKS.

"I'm afraid so, Antonia. I figure that should give us enough time to get to know each other. I usually don't go in for longer relationships, but with you, I think I could be persuaded to change my mind."

In spite of her fury, Toni managed to keep calm. "I appreciate your consideration, Christian. It does something for a woman's morale to be told she's next in line as 'mistress of the month' for someone as infamous as you. However, you'll have to clear all the minor details with my cousin. She's bent on marrying me off within the next few months. Have a good night," she threw over her shoulder as she left the room.

CANDLELIGHT ECSTASY ROMANCES®

250 SUMMER WINE, *Alexis Hill Jardan*
251 NO LOVE LOST, *Eleanor Woods*
252 A MATTER OF JUDGMENT, *Emily Elliott*
253 GOLDEN VOWS, *Karen Whittenburg*
254 AN EXPERT'S ADVICE, *JoAnne Bremer*
255 A RISK WORTH TAKING, *Jan Stuart*
256 GAME PLAN, *Sara Jennings*
257 WITH EACH PASSING HOUR, *Emma Bennett*
258 PROMISE OF SPRING, *Jean Hager*
259 TENDER AWAKENING, *Alison Tyler*
260 DESPERATE YEARNING, *Dallas Hamlin*
261 GIVE AND TAKE, *Sheila Paulos*
262 AN UNFORGETTABLE CARESS, *Donna Kimel Vitek*
263 TOMORROW WILL COME, *Megan Lane*
264 RUN TO RAPTURE, *Margot Prince*
265 LOVE'S SECRET GARDEN, *Nona Gamel*
266 WINNER TAKES ALL, *Cathie Linz*
267 A WINNING COMBINATION, *Lori Copeland*
268 A COMPROMISING PASSION, *Nell Kincaid*
269 TAKE MY HAND, *Anna Hudson*
270 HIGH STAKES, *Eleanor Woods*
271 SERENA'S MAGIC, *Heather Graham*
272 A DARING ALLIANCE, *Alison Tyler*
273 SCATTERED ROSES, *Jo Calloway*
274 WITH ALL MY HEART, *Emma Bennett*
275 JUST CALL MY NAME, *Dorothy Ann Bernard*
276 THE PERFECT AFFAIR, *Lynn Patrick*
277 ONE IN A MILLION, *Joan Grove*
278 HAPPILY EVER AFTER, *Barbara Andrews*
279 SINNER AND SAINT, *Prudence Martin*
280 RIVER RAPTURE, *Patricia Markham*
281 MATCH MADE IN HEAVEN, *Melissa Carroll*
282 TO REMEMBER LOVE, *Jo Calloway*
283 EVER A SONG, *Karen Whittenburg*
284 CASANOVA'S MASTER, *Anne Silverlock*
285 PASSIONATE ULTIMATUM, *Emma Bennett*
286 A PRIZE CATCH, *Anna Hudson*
287 LOVE NOT THE ENEMY, *Sara Jennings*
288 SUMMER FLING, *Natalie Stone*
289 AMBER PERSUASION, *Linda Vail*

FORGOTTEN DREAMS

Eleanor Woods

A CANDLELIGHT ECSTASY ROMANCE®

Published by
Dell Publishing Co., Inc.
1 Dag Hammarskjold Plaza
New York, New York 10017

ISBN: 0-440-12653-3

Printed in the United States of America

First printing—December 1984

To Our Readers:

We have been delighted with your enthusiastic response to Candlelight Ecstasy Romances®, and we thank you for the interest you have shown in this exciting series.

In the upcoming months we will continue to present the distinctive, sensuous love stories you have come to expect only from Ecstasy. We look forward to bringing you many more books from your favorite authors and also the very finest work from new authors of contemporary romantic fiction.

As always, we are striving to present the unique, absorbing love stories that you enjoy most—books that are more than ordinary romance.

Your suggestions and comments are always welcome. Please write to us at the address below.

Sincerely,

The Editors
Candlelight Romances
1 Dag Hammarskjold Plaza
New York, N.Y. 10017

CHAPTER ONE

"Don't you think Christian Barr is the most gorgeous hunk of man you've ever seen?" Connie Ward, the scatterbrained but lovable receptionist, asked as she placed a stack of mail on Antonia Grant's desk. "Karen's been closeted with him for almost two hours." She sighed dreamily.

Her gaze lingered on the closed doors of Studio A, jokingly dubbed the VIP room. Several weekly community interest shows were taped there, as well as personal interviews with newsworthy personalities, such as the one Connie was presently drooling over.

"Gee, I can't remember," Toni said innocently, struggling to maintain a straight face as the receptionist stared disbelievingly at her. "Perhaps if you described him to me it might jar my memory. Was he the older, stoop-shouldered man you introduced me to earlier?" she teased.

"If you missed Christian Barr, your mind doesn't need jarring, it needs dynamiting," Connie replied disgustedly.

"Ahh." Toni chuckled, her dark eyes sparkling with amusement. "Don't tell me you've fallen victim to that self-admitted playboy's charm?"

"Of course I have," Connie said simply. "Do you know he has a sister living here? That means there's an excellent possibility that he'll be staying for a while."

"I do know about the sister." Toni nodded, the movement of her head causing the edges of her black hair to brush against her cheek. "But how will that help you?"

For Connie, collecting men was no mere hobby; it was a vocation that she pursued with almost single-minded dedication. Her only rule was never to go out with married or engaged men. Otherwise, it was always open season and she was always a huntress.

At that moment Steven Crowell, general manager of WSAM-TV and Toni's fiancé, came into the room. "Two beautiful women to welcome me," he said, flashing them his most captivating smile. "The perfect way to start a day." He walked past Connie and around the desk to where Toni was sitting and dropped a light kiss on her upturned face.

"It must be nice to be the owner's son and not have to worry about keeping regular hours," Connie remarked, eyeing the wall clock, which read ten thirty. She followed her little dig with a pert grin.

For a brief moment a flash of anger was visible in Steven's eyes, only to be quickly replaced by his usual smiling expression. "Jealous, Connie?" he asked as he turned to face her.

"Certainly," the attractive blonde said bluntly. "Why can't we all be so lucky as to have a wealthy father?"

"I agree," Toni said, joining in the teasing. "In order for us less important people to draw our paychecks, we have to be here at eight and put in a full day's work."

Steven laughed. "I'll have to see what I can do. It's very important in any organization to see that the employees are kept happy." He started toward his private office. As he reached out to open the door, he turned. "By the way, Toni, I'm afraid we'll have to cancel our date this evening. Dad's tied up and asked me to keep an appointment for him."

"Again?" Toni said, disappointed. It was the third time in a week that their plans had been interrupted because of business.

"I know." Steven shrugged his broad shoulders, a rough sigh escaping his sensuous lips. "But I'll make it up to you, I promise. Come up with something really fantastic for the weekend and we'll slip away and not tell a living soul where we're going."

With the closing of the door, Toni turned back to Connie, her lips tight with resignation. "I certainly hope 'Dad' doesn't suddenly remember some darned appointment on the day of our wedding."

"Perhaps Steven should be more assertive with his father," Connie casually suggested. "After all, he is thirty years old, not three."

"My sentiments exactly," Toni said with a frown. "It's becoming very annoying, having our plans canceled over and over again because the boss can't keep his appointments straight."

"Well, since you're obviously not going to be busy this evening, why not come with Mark and me?" Connie asked. "There's this new restaurant about thirty miles out of town and the food is supposed to be fabulous."

"Don't tell me you've been seeing Mark lately?" Toni asked, incredulous.

"Yes, silly, but it's not what you think. You know Mark's just like a big brother to me."

Why not go? Toni thought as the endless hours of another evening alone flashed through her mind. If she couldn't be with Steven, then good friends certainly seemed the next best thing.

"What time shall I be ready?"

"Sevenish."

After chatting a few minutes longer, Connie left and Toni was alone. Instead of immediately attending to the stack of work on her desk, she sat back in her chair, a thoughtful expression on her face as she considered the direction her life had taken in the last few months.

Since she'd been a freshman in high school, she'd dreamed of a career in television. Never once had she wavered from that decision during the years it took to get a degree in communications. After graduation, and several months at an unexciting job with a radio station, she'd felt fortunate in landing a job with WSAM-TV.

Richmond wasn't that far from the small Virginia town where she'd grown up, and the station wasn't so large that she would become lost in a faceless crowd of employees.

She'd accepted early on that the career she'd chosen was a very competitive one and that all newcomers must pay their dues, so Toni was contented in the beginning to be a sort of jack-of-all-trades and master of none. That suited her just fine; she was learning the business from the ground up, and gaining a wealth of experience that would help her build a solid career.

She smiled as she remembered the first time she'd conducted an interview. It had been with a local author, and after the ordeal was over she'd celebrated with Connie. They'd laughed till tears ran down their faces at the ridiculous posturing of the man. He was a native of Richmond who'd written two books that, while not on the best-seller list, had done reasonably well. The interview had been somewhat of a struggle, but Toni had handled it like a pro. Afterward the congratulations had her floating rather than walking down the halls of the station.

Gradually she began to substitute for other announcers as well as create her own niche in the establishment by doing special stories and interviews. By the time she was twenty-five her face had become well known in the area and she was warmly received by the viewers.

She was on her way, her sights set eventually on the nation's capital or New York, when tragedy struck. While out for a drive with her parents, she was involved in an automobile accident that took the lives of both her mother and father and left Toni with a broken leg, a broken arm, and several fractured ribs.

In less than ten seconds the world Toni had known all her life had been shattered into a million pieces.

Friends rallied to support her through her grief and her own long recuperation. Her only remaining close family, a cousin and one great-aunt who lived some distance away, offered their comfort as well; and, ironically enough, it was the letters from her aunt, Sara Cartlaigne, that eventually made Toni accept her parents' death and get on with the future.

Aunt Sara, ninety-six and, as Toni's father had often said, "hell on wheels," didn't merely wish her niece a speedy recovery. That crotchety old lady *demanded* that she recover. "Don't let those damn fool doctors keep you shackled to a bed longer than is absolutely necessary, Antonia," the matriarch of the Cartlaigne family wrote in her spidery script. She also threatened to travel to Richmond herself if sufficient progress hadn't been made by such and such a date.

As Toni improved physically, her relationship with Steven deepened. They'd dated fairly regularly prior to the accident, and afterward it seemed the most natural thing in the world for her to turn to him. As Toni tried to put her life back in order, Steven's strength and thoughtfulness made him seem a secure haven, the one unchanging thing in her world.

Steven's parents liked Toni and encouraged the steadily developing relationship between her and their son. When Steven asked her to marry him, the elder Crowells seemed every bit as thrilled as the engaged couple, and they hosted a large party to announce the event to their friends.

That had been four months ago, Toni thought warmly. Four months in which she'd been surrounded by Steven's love. The only unpleasant note had been that lately his responsibilities at the station had been steadily increasing, keeping him away from her more and more.

Perhaps, she decided as she tried to smother her disappointment, Steven's father was looking ahead to retirement and wanted to guide his son through the transition of power with as little upheaval as possible.

The morning passed with only a few annoying problems. Toni took care of the ones she could and directed the others to Steven. Since her return to the station, she'd been working as his secretary. Her injured leg had taken a long time to heal, and her doctor had warned her not to return too quickly to her former hectic schedule.

As luck would have it, Steven's secretary had left to have a baby, and Toni had been able to step into that position. Her visits to the hospital as an outpatient for physical therapy dropped from four forty-five-minute sessions each week to three, and then to two. Since her final visit to the therapist was at three thirty, Toni began to tidy her desk at three, then went in to tell Steven she was leaving.

"You can't imagine how tired I am of having our lives run by this monster of a business," he murmured against the softness of her hair as he held her close to him. "I'm longing to be with you, to be able to kiss you in privacy and not worry about someone opening the door to my office and catching us."

"I know," Toni whispered as she stood on tiptoe to tease the curve of his jaw with her lips. "But it won't be forever, sweetheart. Soon we'll be together all the time." She smiled up into his eyes.

"It can't happen soon enough to please me," he said. He sighed roughly against her mouth, then let his lips close over hers in a kiss that had Toni's senses reeling as she clung to him for support.

Neither of them heard the knock on the door nor the steps muffled by the thick carpet as a man and a woman walked into the office. The woman stared with amused indulgence at the couple. She leaned one slim hip against a heavy chair and crossed her arms over her chest, her head cocked at a comical tilt.

There was a curious glint in the tall, powerfully built man's blue eyes as he came upon the embracing couple. His expression shifted from bored acceptance to grim alertness as he quickly examined the small slender woman sharing the lingering kiss. Christian Barr, whose fame as a journalist was exceeded only by his renown as a womanizer, had seen Toni upon his arrival at the station and had felt that familiar stirring within him that occurred whenever he happened upon a woman who caught his attention. He had let his seasoned eye travel appreciatively over dark shining hair and downward, past small breasts, a tiny waist, slim hips, and shapely legs.

There had been something about this woman that had made it unusually difficult for him to concentrate on business. He kept imagining himself seated across from his latest "find" in some cozy restaurant while he calmly and methodically planned her seduction. He wasn't prepared for the indifferent glance Toni had thrown him when Connie became aware of his presence, or of her cool smile as introductions were made. Before he had time to make a single charming remark, Toni had excused herself and walked away, leaving him with a tongue-tied Connie, who by then was ready to throw herself at his feet.

Now he'd found the icy Miss Grant again, but she had apparently thawed quite a bit in so brief a time. The only problem was, Christian thought distastefully, he wasn't the one responsible for melting the ice.

Karen threw him a cheeky grin, then cleared her throat in a manner that would have halted traffic on Main Street in any city. Toni and Steven sprang apart as though jerked in opposite directions by invisible ropes. As Toni swung around, the first thing she saw was the cynical gleam in Christian Barr's blue eyes and the barest twist of his lips. There was something in his expression that made her feel somehow shabby at being caught in her fiancé's arms, she realized as she felt her face turn bright red.

She dropped her gaze after only the briefest contact with his, turning her attention to a teasing Karen, who was apologizing for barging in.

"But we did knock," Karen said with a chuckle, then went on to introduce Steven and Christian.

As the two men moved forward to shake hands Toni couldn't help but notice that Christian Barr was several inches taller than Steven. He also appeared older, she decided, considering the weathered toughness of his rough-hewn features and the tiny lines that fanned out from his eyes. His hair was dark and thick, as were the heavy brows that grew above his piercing eyes. For no reason at all, Toni found herself resenting the man. He had an air about him that set her on edge. It was as though he felt superior to the people around him.

Without going to a great deal of trouble to hide her own assessment of the man, Toni excused herself and left the room. There was no denying the fact that Christian Barr was news wherever he went, she thought as she scooped up her purse and headed out of the building and to her car.

His name had become synonymous with excellence in the field of journalism, particularly in investigative reporting. No corrupt organization, federal program, or public figure was beyond his reach if unfortunate enough to catch his attention. According to articles written about him, Toni knew he'd been threatened by a number of the people he'd gone after. He'd had a couple of lawsuits brought against him, which he'd won, and he'd actually been shot at on one occasion.

"Add that to his colorful social life and you've got quite a character," Toni muttered as she got into her car. Almost the only redeeming quality she could think of at the moment regarding the infamous Mr. Barr was his reluctance to marry. At least he was kind enough not to inflict himself permanently on some poor woman. Toni had no trouble at all imagining the sort of life a wife of his would lead.

As she had hoped, her final session with the therapist was brief and in no time at all Toni was on her way to her apartment to shower and dress for the evening.

By the time her friends arrived to pick her up, Toni had managed to mask her disappointment at not being able to see Steven that evening.

The restaurant Connie and Mark were so anxious to try turned out to be picturesque and served excellent food. But it was the overnight accommodations that caught Toni's eye.

Rather than building a conventional motel, the architect had carefully designed a number of one- and two-bedroom cottages to blend in with the lush trees that grew so abundantly in the area. A small stream meandered lazily through the grounds toward an old grist mill that was still standing, its huge wooden wheel intact. Though the wheel was no longer used for its original purpose and was made to turn by electricity, the effect was still the same.

The setting was rustic and appealing and made Toni feel as if she had been transported to some other, more romantic time. This fact did not go unnoticed by Mark and Connie as they observed the rapt expression on her face.

She endured their good-natured comments in the same vein as they were offered. "Well, at least the owners have tried to retain the natural beauty of the area," she said with a shrug as they turned and walked toward the entrance to the restaurant. "But I suppose you'd like it better if a kidney-shaped pool replaced the stream and the music of some punk rock band was blaring over the speakers," she said to Connie.

"For once I agree with you," the blonde replied with an easy grin. "Not that I'd care to spend more than a day or two here, mind you."

The two of them continued their friendly bickering as they entered the restaurant, but stopped short when Mark announced his disappointment at the shocking lack of scantily clad beauties milling about carrying tall, frosted glasses of alcoholic beverages.

"Philistine!" Connie hissed at him.

"Unappreciative pig," Toni said with a chuckle. "Endless orgies and a continuous flow of mind-numbing liquor. That's all you want."

"Exactly." Mark nodded his blond head, a mischievous expression on his attractive features. "What more could a man possibly ask for?"

Both women slowly shook their heads, each muttering her own thoughts regarding his depraved character, and began to inspect the menu. They retaliated by ordering the most expensive dishes offered, then sat back and laughed when Mark almost fainted at the thought of the check. They let him suffer several minutes before telling him that the evening was Dutch treat.

As they ate, Toni couldn't help but wish that Steven were seated next to her. She felt almost guilty for enjoying herself while he was stuck in a dull meeting, attempting to work out the complicated details of some business deal his father wanted. It didn't seem fair.

She was about to say just that when Connie gave a loud gasp, then stared across the room as Mark began to talk at a rate of speed that would have made any auctioneer jealous.

Toni looked curiously at one and then the other. "Have you suddenly seen a ghost?" she asked Connie, noting the shocked expression on her friend's face.

"No." Connie quickly shook her head, a nervous laugh escaping her. "It's nothing. . . . I . . . er . . ." Before her stammering explanation could be completed, Toni glanced up as a couple was being shown to a table near the large windows that overlooked the grounds.

She froze.

The fork that was raised halfway to her mouth with its tiny wedge of tomato was slowly lowered to her plate. The couple that held her undivided attention was none other than Steven and a tall, attractive redhead.

Toni watched along with Connie and Mark as Steven reached for his companion's hand and raised it to his lips in a lingering kiss. Instead of releasing her after such an obvious show of affection, Steven kept his fingers intertwined with hers as if he couldn't bear not to touch her.

Toni could clearly see the warmth and softness in his face, and, she told herself, it certainly didn't require an expert on human emotions to see that these two were much more than "business" acquaintances.

It took all of her willpower to pull her gaze away from Steven. She looked at Mark and Connie, an expression of shock and disbelief on her face.

Mark glanced at Connie, who gave him a hurried nod. He removed his napkin from his lap and placed it beside his plate. "Why don't you ladies go on to the car? I'll pay the check and be right with you."

"Great!" Connie exclaimed a little too enthusiastically as she began to scramble beneath her chair for her purse. "Do hurry, Mark. I've suddenly taken a distinct dislike to this place."

"No." The one word slipped softly but firmly past Toni's lips. "Why should we deprive ourselves of a delicious dinner just because Steven has been caught playing footsie?"

"Oh . . . but, honey," Connie cried in a low voice. "This must be awful for you. I never dreamed they'd be . . . I mean . . ." She stopped her helpless jabbering and looked imploringly at Mark.

"I think what Connie's trying to say is that we're just as shocked as you are, Toni," he said smoothly. "And we can certainly understand your wanting to leave."

But Toni had caught Connie's slip of the tongue. She reached for her wineglass with an amazingly steady hand and raised it to her lips. The cool liquid offered only minimal relief to her parched mouth. "I don't think that's what Connie meant at all, Mark, and neither do you. I get the distinct impression that the two of you know more than you're telling me."

She included them both in a shrewd look, her dark eyes going back and forth from one uncomfortable expression to the other. "Well? Are you going to sit there and deny that you know Steven has been seeing other women behind my back? Or are you going to tell me the truth?"

"Oh, Lord," Connie mumbled, shaking her head in disbelief. "This can't be happening."

"But it is, and I want to know for how long," Toni said bluntly. "In the last two months I've spent more time with the two of you than I have with Steven. I believed his stories about long business meetings. But from the looks of his present dinner companion, I'd say that I've been royally had."

"All right." Mark gave a deep sigh of concern. He took hold of Toni's clenched hand and held it in his warm grasp. "This isn't the first time we've seen them together." He shrugged. "I suppose Steven assumed that since Connie and I work at the station and might be concerned for our jobs, we would think twice before telling you."

"Was that the reason you kept quiet, Mark?" Toni asked softly.

"No," he said firmly. "I'm a damn good cameraman, honey, and I've never had any trouble finding a job. But Connie and I talked it over and decided that with everything that's happened to you during the past year, you didn't need to be told that your fiancé was two-timing you."

"Do other people at the station know?"

"I doubt it. He has been discreet, I will say that for him. It's just that once before Connie and I ran into him and Lea in a nightclub."

"Lea? Is that her name?" Toni asked calmly. *How strange,* she thought as she sat listening to Mark, *that I can sit here as though nothing more disturbing than a light shower of rain has dared to intrude on this peaceful evening.* Deeper introspection would come later. She knew that. At the moment, however, she felt nothing but a kind of self-protective numbness separating her from the harsh reality of what she was seeing and hearing. That, and a deep brooding anger.

"Her name is Lea Simmons. Her family owns several radio stations in the state," Mark answered.

"Do you suppose Steven is attempting to work out some sort of merger?" Toni asked acidly.

"That . . . I can't say. In fact, I'm not even sure the woman knows he's engaged," Mark pointed out.

"Well." Toni removed her hand from Mark's, sat straighter in her chair, then smiled at her friends. "I'm ready for dessert. Oh . . . and Mark," she said pleasantly, "why don't we have a bottle of champagne sent over to the happy couple? I'll pay for it, of course. I think it would add the perfect touch to a most spectacular evening, don't you?"

CHAPTER TWO

"Oh, my." Connie stared round-eyed at Toni. "Are you sure you wouldn't rather leave quietly and talk to Steven about this little incident later?" she asked pleadingly.

"If you're afraid that what I do will cause some trouble for you and Mark, Connie, then I'll simply have the waiter find me a separate table. I can also call a taxi to take me home."

"Oh, honey, it isn't that," Connie said unhappily. She was clearly rattled by this sudden turn of events, and more than a little concerned by the way Toni was behaving.

It just didn't seem normal for a woman to catch her fiancé with another woman, then send over champagne while she calmly ate and watched.

Mark patted Connie soothingly on the shoulder. *Damn!* he thought. *I'd like to choke Steven Crowell. I've got one woman on my hands about to go into hysterics, while the other one is as calm and beady-eyed as an executioner.* And yet, there was something about the way Toni was handling this thing that he admired. His only relief was that he wasn't the two-timing jerk over by the window.

The waiter was duly summoned and the order for champagne given.

"Any message?" the young man asked.

"Er . . . I don't think—"

"Yes," Toni interrupted Mark, smiling sweetly at the waiter. "How about . . . 'Compliments of Toni.' Don't you think that has a nice ring to it?" she asked Mark and Connie. She turned back to the young man. "I think that will do nicely." On Toni's insistence they also ordered dessert; then the three of them sat back, watching and waiting, lost in their own thoughts.

Connie seemed near a state of collapse. Her hands were shaking visibly as she lifted her wineglass to her lips. She swallowed the entire contents in one gulp, then lowered the glass to the table and pushed it toward Mark. "A refill?" she croaked.

Mark chuckled softly and did as requested. He'd been happy in Richmond, he thought fleetingly. But what the hell. . . . He was single and free to go and do as he pleased. There'd be no trouble finding another job. He'd cast his lot with Toni, and he would stand by her.

Toni, on the other hand, began to eat her dessert as soon as the waiter set it before her. The only thought running through her mind, other than the thought of confronting Steven, was a curiosity as to why she'd suddenly developed such an enormous appetite. Then a surreptitious glance in Connie's direction brought a sobering expression to Toni's face. Connie and Mark were good friends, caught in a situation they'd had nothing to do with. She certainly had no desire to see them punished for something she was about to do.

"Why don't the two of you leave?" She posed the question seriously, hoping they would understand that she wasn't expecting them to blindly follow her.

"No," the answer came, swiftly and firmly.

It was only one word, but to Toni it was as if she had been alone on a battlefield, then suddenly turned and discovered that an entire battalion had materialized behind her.

Out of the corner of her eye she caught sight of the waiter making his way toward the two lovebirds by the window. With the barely audible murmur of "I think Steven is about to receive the biggest surprise of his life," she nodded toward her fiancé, then let one small, slim hand ease forward and lightly grasp the stem of her wineglass.

She watched alertly as the waiter approached the table, spoke in low-voiced conversation to Steven and Lea Simmons, then turned and gestured toward Toni, who raised her glass in a silent salute.

For what seemed like an eternity the shocked man stared disbelievingly into the dark, expressive eyes of the woman several tables away. Where once there'd been a never-ending flow of warmth and love for him, Steven now saw anger, distrust, and sadness. He dropped his gaze and turned back to the attractive woman seated opposite him.

Without thinking of what she was about to say or do, Toni rose to her feet and glided across the room till she was standing beside Steven.

"What a lovely surprise," she said easily, despite the hard, cold hand clutching her heart. She looked from her tongue-tied fiancé to Lea Simmons. "Since Steven seems to have misplaced his manners, it looks as though I'll have to introduce myself. My name is Toni Grant."

"Hello, Toni. I'm Lea Simmons. You must be a friend of Steven's. Thanks so much for the champagne. It was such a sweet idea," the redhead said pleasantly, and Toni knew immediately that Lea Simmons was as much a victim of circumstances as she.

"You could say that. Actually I'm his secretary." Toni directed her gaze toward a grim-faced Steven, who was sitting as though turned to stone. "Did your 'business' meeting go well, Steven?"

"Yes," he said shortly. "It went as planned."

"Don't you just love this place, Miss Simmons?" Toni asked warmly. "This is my first time, but I'll be coming back every chance I get."

"It is beautiful," Lea agreed. "Steven has been promising to bring me here for weeks. I must say, though, the wait was worth it."

"Shame on you," Toni said to her fiancé. She reached out as though to tap him on the wrist. But instead of an innocuous flick of her fingers against his tanned skin, she slipped them beneath the edge of his soup bowl and tipped the steaming liquid directly into his lap.

"Oh, dear!" Toni exclaimed in feigned horror at her supposed clumsiness as her victim shot to his feet like a bolt of lightning. "Just look what I've done."

"Think nothing of it," Steven snapped. He was wiping frantically at the front of his pants while muttering a number of rather colorful oaths.

Toni threw the astounded Lea an apologetic look. "I'm so sorry for ruining your evening. But perhaps you can get Steven to bring you back. I know for a fact that he'll have more free time on his hands starting in the very near future." Without another word, she turned on her heel and walked back to the table where Mark and Connie stood waiting.

"Feeling better?" Mark grinned as he stepped to one side of her and took her arm. He motioned Connie to the other side, then shepherded his party from the room.

"Much," Toni said faintly.

"Will our . . . er . . . esteemed leader need medical attention?"

"He might. The soup was giving up spirals of smoke like Indians sending signals."

"You don't think he's seriously burned, do you?" a tenderhearted Connie asked.

"I sincerely hope so, Connie. I sincerely hope so," Toni said without the slightest hint of compassion softening her voice.

The drive back to town and to her apartment was one of the longest Toni had ever made in her life. Now that those first explosive moments of shock had been dealt with and her anger had cooled somewhat, she felt numb.

Mark and Connie tried to keep a conversation going, but after getting no response from Toni on several occasions, they too lapsed into a moody silence.

When Mark stopped the car in front of Toni's apartment building, he turned off the engine and reached for the door handle.

"Don't," Toni said quietly. "There's no need for you to get out." She smiled. "What I need at the moment is a cup of hot tea and some time to think."

"Are you sure?" Connie asked. "I'd be happy to spend the night with you."

"I know you would, but I honestly think I'd rather be alone."

"Will you be in tomorrow?"

"I'll be in," Toni said firmly. She opened the door and stepped out, then turned and smiled at her two friends. "Don't look so worried. A year from now we'll look back on this evening and have a good laugh."

The words were brave and Toni wanted to believe them. But as she let herself into her apartment, she couldn't help but think of the old cliché about talk being cheap.

She made her way to the bedroom, where she took off her dress, then slipped into a pair of comfortable old pajamas. Her movements were mechanical and, at the moment, so were her thoughts. It wasn't until she was in the kitchen waiting for the water to boil for her tea that the events of the evening began to seem real.

The man she'd trusted with her heart, the same man she'd planned to spend her life with, had betrayed her.

She was amazed that her eyes were still dry. *Why?* she asked herself over and over again as she fixed the tea, then carried it to the living room where she curled up on the sofa. *Why can't I cry?* But no answer presented itself.

From the moment she'd looked up and seen Steven and Lea in the restaurant till she'd tipped the bowl of hot soup in his lap, the only emotions she'd felt had been shock and anger.

She looked at the diamond solitaire she wore on her left hand. Perhaps the redheaded Lea wouldn't mind a secondhand ring.

Without thinking, Toni removed the ring and slowly moved it back and forth, watching the brilliant fire it gave off as the light of the table lamp caught the many facets of the stone. It was beautiful.

She remembered the evening Steven had given it to her and the words he'd spoken as he slipped it on her finger. "Now I can stop worrying that some other man will steal you away from me," he'd whispered. "This is my brand on you, Antonia Grant. And soon there'll be a band of gold to wholly make you mine."

He'd kissed her then, passionately and hungrily, until Toni finally pulled back, preventing them from consummating their vows prematurely.

She frowned. Could that pulling back and the fact that she'd continued to do so during the months afterward have been a warning in itself? Or could she have known on some level that Steven's behavior—the outbursts of temper, the canceled dates, the moody silences—meant that he was hiding his real feelings from her and that he couldn't be trusted?

The questions continued, swirling in her head until she almost became dizzy from trying to sort them out. Finally she gave up and went to bed, having made only one definite decision. She would resign her job at the television station.

As the first gentle pull of sleep touched her eyelids, Toni was jarred awake by the shrill ringing of the phone.

It was probably Steven, she told herself as she sat up in bed and stared at the lighted dial of the phone on the bedside table. Nothing on earth could induce her to speak to him this evening.

She reached out and lifted the receiver and immediately heard his voice calling her name. Very calmly, and with a definiteness of purpose that surprised even her, Toni depressed the button to break the connection, then unplugged the phone.

As Toni swept into the front door of the station the next morning, there was little evidence to indicate that she'd only gotten three or four hours of sleep the night before.

The skillful application of makeup to hide the circles beneath her eyes, and the determination not to become an object of pity among her co-workers, had her looking her usual attractive self. Even her clothes, a deep cranberry skirt and a matching silk blouse, had been chosen because they were stylish and cheerful.

Connie, whose desk faced the door, glanced up as Toni entered, a concerned look on her face.

"Good morning." Toni smiled as she paused to assure the other woman that all was well.

"Are you okay?" Connie immediately asked, getting right to the point.

"I'm fine, and you're not to worry," said Toni. "I realize it's a silly question, but is Steven in yet?"

"He got here before I did. Can you believe it?"

"Has he said anything to you about what happened?" Toni asked curiously. "Was he abrupt with you in any way?"

Connie shrugged. "He nodded when we passed in the hall. Other than that, I haven't seen him."

"If you can possibly avoid it, don't put through any calls to him for a while, okay?" Toni asked.

"Sure thing. And if you need any help, just yell." Connie grinned. "I'll keep one ear trained in the direction of his office."

Toni walked through her office and past her desk, pausing only when she reached the door to Steven's domain. She raised a fist and knocked. At his bid to enter, she opened the door and stepped inside, then closed the door behind her.

"Toni!" he exclaimed, jumping to his feet and hurrying around his desk toward her. When he was within arm's reach his hands shot out to grasp her shoulders. Toni neatly avoided his touch and stepped around him.

"Good morning, Steven," she said as she walked over to his desk. She opened her purse and removed a long, slim, velvet-covered box containing a bracelet he'd given her for her birthday, and a tiny square box that held her engagement ring.

"What are you doing?" he asked nervously. He'd followed and was now standing beside her.

"I'm returning your bracelet and your engagement ring, Steven." She looked up at him, her expression unreadable. "Under the circumstances, don't you think it's best that we break our engagement?"

"What for?" he asked sulkily. He ran one hand around the back of his neck, then walked over to the window and stared out.

"What for?" Toni repeated. "I think that should be obvious. You're not ready for marriage. My ideas regarding marriage are simple, Steven. I believe in a man and woman who love each other exchanging vows and staying faithful to each other till death them do part. I really don't care for your idea of having a spare female stashed away in case you decide you need a change in the menu."

"That's not a very nice thing to say about the man you love," he snapped as he swung around to face her. "Maybe if you had been a little more affectionate I wouldn't have had to go elsewhere."

Toni leaned one hip against the edge of the desk and regarded him thoughtfully. "That's very convenient. What you're really saying is that if I'd gone to bed with you, then you wouldn't have gone out with other women?"

"Who the hell told you about the others? Was it that nosy broad Connie?" he snarled.

"Connie and Mark had nothing to do with me learning about the little games you've been playing. But it doesn't take a great deal of intelligence to figure you out. The only thing I regret is that Lea Simmons seems like a nice girl. It's a shame she's had the misfortune of becoming involved with a rat like you."

With that, Toni swung around and headed for the door. She'd heard and seen enough. In fact, she told herself, she'd learned more about Steven Crowell in the last twenty-four hours than she had in all the months since she'd first met him.

Before she could open the door, however, Steven was beside her, one long arm slipping in front of her, his other hand catching hold of her elbow. "You can't walk out on me like this, Toni," he said in the deep, persuasive voice she used to think so appealing. "I made a mistake . . . several of them, honey, but it's you I love. It's you I want to spend the rest of my life with."

Toni stared incredulously at him, disliking him more with each passing second. It was becoming increasingly clear to her that Steven could lie as easily as most people breathed.

"I'm sorry, Steven, but my mind's made up. I could never trust you again. Can't you understand that?"

"Of course I can," he hurriedly agreed. "I've hurt you and you're striking back. That's understandable.

But if you'll just bear with me, I'll prove you can trust me."

"But you're missing the point, Steven," she said firmly, determined not to let her temper get the upper hand, as it had the evening before. "I don't want to bear with you, nor do I intend to work for you any longer. I'll be handing in my resignation at the end of the day."

"I won't accept it." He smiled suggestively, as if that simple statement would make everything all right again.

"Then I'd suggest you reconsider, Steven. You *need* a secretary," she said crisply. Then she reached beneath his arm for the doorknob, leaving Steven no choice but to step aside. Instead of leaving her alone for the moment and letting tempers cool, he followed Toni into her office.

"I'd suggest you reconsider, Toni," he said sneeringly. "I'm not likely to give a glowing recommendation to an employee who thinks she can walk out on me with only a moment's notice."

Toni wheeled around to face him, sparks of anger visible in the depths of her dark eyes. "Are you by any chance threatening me?" she asked icily.

"Consider it what you will. Just remember, though, you signed a contract that stated you would give two weeks' notice unless some unusual circumstance prevented your doing so. From where I stand it looks as though the present 'circumstance' is nothing more than a temper tantrum," Steven said harshly.

"Oh? Is that what it's called these days when a two-timing jerk is caught red-handed? A temper tantrum?" Toni lashed out, her tiny frame literally shaking with rage.

Steven's face turned beet red at the accusation. "We'll discuss this later, when you've gotten that damnable temper under control and have realized that whatever embarrassment you might have suffered is a small price to pay for being Mrs. Steven Crowell."

He started to turn away, then paused. "And while you're reconsidering your future, you'd better get with your friend Mark. Karen is ill today and you'll have to do the noon weather spot."

"Weather?" Toni shouted as her fingers closed around a vase of cut flowers Steven had given her a couple of days ago after having broken another date. "I'll be happy to give you the most current meteorlogical update available. Let's start with rain, shall we?" she cried, then picked up the vase and flung the entire contents in his face.

Completely out of control now she threw the vase into a corner of the room, where it shattered into a million pieces. "Did you hear the thunder?" she yelled. "I'll be happy to repeat the forecast at noon if you insist."

"Why, you little bitch," Steven snarled. He reached out for Toni, only to be stopped by a commanding voice from the doorway.

"I don't think I'd do that if I were you," Christian Barr said in a menacing tone that brought Steven to an abrupt standstill and had the hair on Toni's neck standing on end.

Both combatants turned and stared at the huge man whose width and height seemed to fill every available inch of space in the doorway.

Toni saw a pair of blue eyes glittering like steel points as they pinned Steven. His stance was loose, and one long arm was braced against the doorjamb.

He reminded her of some large animal of prey, waiting, biding his time before the attack. She also had a gut feeling that if Steven so much as blinked, Christian Barr would put that incredible force emanating from him into very definite action.

"This is none of your business, Barr," Steven said tightly. His fists were clenched at his sides and his face was livid.

"I agree. But regardless, I don't go in for hitting women. I don't mind a fight, but I've always thought it more challenging if my opponent were less fragile than yours appears to be."

Steven stared angrily at the determined intruder for several seconds, then swung his chilling gaze to Toni. "I'll accept your resignation, Miss Grant," he snapped. "Clean out your desk and be off the premises in exactly one hour." With one last flinty glare at Christian Barr, Steven turned and barreled his way into his office and slammed the door behind him.

Toni briefly closed her eyes and ran a slim hand up to clasp the nape of her neck. She felt as though she'd just gotten off a roller coaster, flying out of control up and down the longest track in the world.

When a large, warm hand clasped her shoulder, she jumped and opened her eyes to find Christian Barr standing directly in front of her.

"Are you all right?" he asked with concern.

"Y-yes." She nodded, staring intently at the striking features of her rescuer. As she concentrated on this close study it flashed through her mind that his face seemed to reflect the sort of exciting cloak-and-dagger life he lived.

There were a couple of tiny niches along the edge of his square chin, a small scar at his hairline, and another over one dark brow. His nose, which she was certain had to have been straight at one time, now had a decided bump midway. She could well imagine the sort of "activity" that had produced such a slight disfigurement.

It was his mouth, though, that fascinated her most, with its thin upper lip and the fuller, more sensuous bottom one. Her gaze lingered thoughtfully until some slight movement from Christian broke the spell.

"I think you should call your friend Connie," he said quietly but commandingly.

"There really isn't that much to pack," Toni said as she turned to her desk and put several feet between them. Wow! she was thinking. No wonder Christian Barr was so adored by the ladies. He played the role of the gallant protector to perfection. She could just see him, hypnotizing his victims into a state of well-being, then pouncing on them when they least expected it.

Well, this is one female he won't get a chance at, she congratulated herself. *I've just been exposed to what can happen when a woman gives her heart to a man with a roving eye. And compared to Christian Barr, Steven is still in kindergarten.*

CHAPTER THREE

Connie, hearing the commotion and becoming concerned for Toni, chose that moment to put in an appearance.

"Oh, my!" she exclaimed as she stepped just inside Toni's office and looked at the large wet spot on the carpet, the scattered flowers, and the shattered vase. "Oh, my!" she exclaimed again more softly as she turned startled eyes toward Toni and Christian Barr.

"It's all right, Connie." Toni smiled at her friend. "It looks far worse than it is, I assure you." She opened a drawer and began to take out her personal articles. "Could you possibly find me a box? Oh . . . and would you call the janitor and ask him to clean up this mess? I'm afraid the weather's been rather stormy."

"Of course," Connie replied faintly, then slowly backed out of the room, a look of disbelief still on her face.

"I think you've thoroughly shocked your friend," Christian said with a chuckle. Without asking permission, he sat on one corner of her desk, then locked his hands around one knee and leaned back. "May I be so bold as to ask what brought about this . . . er . . . altercation between you and your fiancé?"

"Ex-fiancé, and no, you may not ask. Why should it interest you?" Toni asked as she continued to remove her things from the desk.

"Simple," Christian told her. "You're a beautiful woman and I have a great interest in beautiful women."

Toni paused, giving him a narrowed look from beneath dark brows. "Somehow, Mr. Barr, that very flattering little speech fails to do a single thing for me."

She returned to her task, either side of her generous mouth bracketed with annoyance. "I appreciate your timely intervention a few minutes ago, but now that you've done your good deed for the day, would you mind leaving? As you obviously heard and can see, I have quite a bit to do and a very short time in which to do it."

"Oh, don't mind me." Christian smiled brazenly. "I'll just sit here, quiet as a little mouse."

"Hmmm." Toni frowned. "Quiet you may be. But little? Hardly."

Damn the man! Was he so insensitive as to be getting some perverted pleasure from her present situation? Couldn't he see that she wanted to be alone?

Connie's reappearance with a box was a much welcomed intrusion. She sat the cardboard container on the desk, her eyes darting from Toni to a smiling Christian. "There was no possible way to work things out?" she finally asked.

Toni looked pointedly at the end results of the conversation between her and Steven, then shrugged. "I do believe the lines of communication have been irrevocably cut. In fact"—she pushed back her cuff and glanced at her watch—"I have exactly forty-five minutes to pack and leave."

"I'm in need of a secretary," Christian Barr informed Toni with a devilish grin. "You could name your hours, plus travel extensively."

"No thanks," Toni said, then regarded him suspiciously. "I've always been leery of jobs with glowing fringe benefits."

"Maybe you should think about Mr. Barr's offer, Toni," Connie said. "Jobs aren't that easy to come by these days."

Toni stared at the receptionist, not believing she'd heard correctly. But Connie was dead serious, her face a study of concern as she pondered Toni's future.

After favoring Christian with a withering look, Toni tried to set Connie's mind at ease. "You do have a point, but I think I need a change of scenery. Aunt Sara has been after me for months to visit her. It's been over three years since I last saw her. Now seems the perfect time to make my favorite relative happy and take a vacation."

"But Natchez, Mississippi, is such a long way from Richmond," Connie said with a frown. "Will you drive or fly?"

"Drive . . . I think," Toni told her, then changed the subject by asking Connie if she would look after her plants while she was away.

Forty-five minutes later, as she placed her purse and the box containing her belongings from her desk on the front seat of her small compact car, Toni looked back toward the building where she'd worked for over two years. She'd made some good friends, and she would miss them, but she knew it was time to move on, to new faces . . . new places.

"I can't beleve it!" Susie cried excitedly. "You're really coming?"

"Of course I am, silly." Toni laughed at her dizzy cousin. "I plan on leaving Richmond around noon tomorrow. I should see you sometime late Friday evening."

"Oh, Toni, this is fantastic. Aunt Sara hasn't been feeling well lately, and I'm sure this will be just the thing to perk her up."

"Aunt Sara's ill? What's wrong?" Toni asked.

"Nothing so bad that she would cancel her weekly afternoon of tea with Miss Louella Rutherford."

"You're kidding."

"Not in the least. Aunt Sara considers Miss Louella a mere child, since she's only eighty and our dear aunt is a very spry ninety-six. But enough about your relatives. . . . Is Steven going to join you during your visit?"

"I doubt it, Susie. He's very . . ." She hesitated, then decided to go on and get it over with. "Steven and I have broken up. As a matter of fact, I handed in my resignation this morning."

"Well, I hope you made the right decision," Susie said after a slight pause, concern evident in her voice. "Would you like me to fly to Richmond and keep you company on the drive?"

"No." Toni smiled. "You stay put and get all your little projects out of the way so that when I arrive, we can gossip for days and days."

After the conversation ended, Toni sat back and stared thoughtfully into space, a slow, gentle warmth stealing over her. She needed her cousin Susie and Susie's fun-loving husband, Brent. She also needed and wanted to be near Aunt Sara, wanted to hear the acid comments from her aged relative that always kept her laughing.

Yes, Toni decided as she roused herself and began to think of the plants she'd need to take over to Connie's, going to Natchez was probably the wisest decision she'd made in months.

Toni parked her car as close as possible to the entrance to Connie's apartment. She got out of the car, then reached for the two ferns nearest her. By the time she got to the door, her arms seemed ready to snap. By shifting her burden so that her view was blocked, she managed to get a finger free and pressed it against the doorbell.

Almost immediately the door opened. "Thank heaven," she muttered as she attempted to juggle the luxurious fronds tickling her nose. "These things weigh—"

Toni stared, speechless. It wasn't Connie who was reaching out and relieving her of the two potted plants, but Christian Barr. He was still wearing the same dark pants and matching knit shirt she'd noticed while he'd been lounging on her desk. But what on earth was he doing at Connie's apartment?

"Why don't you come in?" Christian asked as he stood with a flowing fern balanced in each large hand like some huge landmark, a grin of amusement on his face.

"Oh, no. I . . . that is . . ." Lord! What had she stumbled upon?

"Connie's in the bedroom changing into something

more comfortable." He turned and looked helplessly around the room, then back at Toni. "Where am I supposed to put these things?"

Now that her initial surprise was fading, Toni stepped inside the living room, her eye immediately going to the glass doors that led to the minuscule patio. "Just set them over there." She nodded toward the doors. "The evenings have gotten too cool for them to be outside."

Christian did as she instructed and then straightened to his rather formidable height and walked back to where she was standing.

"Are there more?" he asked, still smiling, his gaze running appreciatively over Toni and the close-fitting jeans and baggy sweatshirt she was wearing.

I wonder how long it's taken him to perfect that smile? she thought. *Maybe his mind is programmed so that even in his sleep he has that seductive expression.*

"Are there more pots . . . plants . . . whatever in your car?" he asked again, then had the unbelievable gall to chuckle when he saw Toni's lips become taut with annoyance.

"Two more," she said coolly, "but I can get them, Mr. Barr, there's no—"

"I'll get them, Miss Grant. Why don't you have a seat? You look as though you aren't feeling well," he said innocently, then left before she could reply.

"I can't believe this," she muttered. "Connie and Christian Barr? She has to be out of her mind."

But at that moment it was a very happy Connie who swept into the room, clad in a soft, clinging jumpsuit with a plunging neckline that caused Toni's jaw to drop.

"Toni!" she cried excitedly. "I'm so glad you finally

got here. I was afraid you'd decided to let someone else look after your babies."

"No . . . I didn't. I . . . Connie," Toni said in a rush, "what on earth is Christian Barr doing here? Are you crazy? That man collects women like small boys collect marbles. Not only that, he admits it."

"I know." Connie laughed, without concern. "Isn't he fantastic? I've never met anyone quite like him before. He's taking me out to dinner."

"Well, just be careful," Toni warned. "Your gentleman might turn into a boa constrictor at the drop of a hat."

"Don't be such a ninny," the pert blonde said airily. "Sit down and let's talk. Have you called your aunt Sara yet?"

Toni perched on the edge of the sofa and, with one wary eye on the door, filled Connie in on her plans.

"Didn't you tell me that the 'big house' next to your aunt's cottage is vacant again?" Connie asked after listening for several minutes.

"It's not exactly vacant. The son of a wealthy newspaper executive bought it for his wife. But after extensive renovations to the first floor, they decided to get a divorce. She's from New Orleans and wasn't happy with the quieter lifestyle that Natchez offered . . . or so my cousin Susie tells me."

"And her husband?"

"He's in New Orleans also." Toni smiled. "His 'daddy' put him in charge of a new magazine they're launching that's supposedly geared to the South and Southwest."

At that moment there was a loud crash outside the door, followed by a gruff male voice letting loose a string of curses. Background for these remarks was amply provided by the frantic barking of a dog.

Both women jumped to their feet and raced to the door. The scene that greeted them was so outrageously funny that they became convulsed with laughter.

Christian Barr was sitting amid the broken remains of a large ceramic pot, with a bountiful supply of dark potting soil liberally heaped on and around him. Toni's weeping fig was leaning precariously over one massive shoulder, and Christian was protectively clutching a pitiful, bedraggled gray kitten to his chest while demanding of a completely shattered woman to "Get that damned dog's leash from around my ankle, madam!"

Without slowing down, he glowered toward Connie and Toni, who were struggling to control the gales of laughter coming from them. "If you two ladies can manage to pull yourselves together, I would appreciate some help," he snapped.

It took several confusing minutes to sort out the mess. The woman to whom Christian had spoken so harshly eventually got her dog untangled, then picked it up and hurried away without a word.

Christian continued to hold and soothe the ugly little kitten while Connie and Toni swept and picked up the potting soil, the broken pot, and the weeping fig.

Once calm prevailed and they were back in Connie's living room, Christian gave Toni a flinty stare. "Miss Grant," he said coldly. "The next time you decide either to break up with your fiancé, resign your position, or go on vacation, would you please post notices on every available bulletin board within a fifty-mile radius? That way, I and other innocent people will be well warned and can stay out of your way."

Toni drew herself up to her full but still short height and haughtily regarded him. "Mr. Barr . . . I don't recall a single moment during the three incidents you've mentioned where I asked for your help. Furthermore, I didn't tell you to referee a cat and dog fight. You did that all on your own." She continued to glare at him for several seconds, then turned to Connie. "I'll call you tomorrow before I leave," she said, and quickly exited.

Toni was lying comfortably against neatly clipped grass. A sprinkling of leaves reminded her that autumn had indeed arrived. She'd been in Natchez for a week now and already she'd fallen victim to the slow, easy pace that was an accepted way of life in the Deep South.

Susie Logan was sitting against a huge oak whose spreading limbs formed a canopy over part of the grounds surrounding Cartlaigne Cottage.

The word *cottage* was a misnomer, Toni thought dreamily as she allowed her gaze to float over the graceful lines of the one-and-a-half-story structure that had been in her family since the 1830s.

The cottage had been a concession of sorts for two old-maid sisters of Joshua Cartlaigne. They hadn't felt welcome when their elder brother remarried after the death of his first wife, so they worked out a plan whereby they would have a separate residence but still remain on the grounds of their childhood home.

Toni couldn't help but smile as she remembered hearing tales handed down through generations about how her aunts bargained with their dominating brother and won. They'd demanded that the line of succession regarding residency of the cottage be passed only to female descendants of the Cartlaigne family who were unmarried. They further stipulated that if the residing female happened to marry during her stay in the cottage, and there were no other single females of legal age, she and her husband could remain—so long as it was understood that the property could only be passed along as the original order stipulated.

"What are you smiling about?" Susie put aside the book she was reading and regarded her cousin with merry eyes.

"The Cartlaigne curse." Toni grinned. "Have you ever considered the fact that our female ancestors didn't exactly set the world on fire when it came to home, hearth, husbands, and babies?"

"I like to think of them as very progressive ladies," Susie said with a laugh. "Does it bother you, Toni? I mean coming back here after a broken engagement. Are you finding this whole scene a little eerie or are you just indulging in humorous stories of the past?"

"The latter, I assure you. Now that I'm away from Steven, I look back and I can't believe how easily I accepted his ring and agreed to marry him."

"Don't you think the accident and your parents' death had a lot to do with your decision?" Susie asked thoughtfully.

"Indeed I do," Toni agreed. "I felt alone . . . was alone, and Steven was there. At the time it seemed the most natural thing in the world to turn to him. I get goose bumps when I think of what could have happened if I hadn't caught him with Lea Simmons."

"From what you told me, poor Steven must have gotten more than goose bumps . . . more like intense pain."

"I can't believe you're wasting your pity on Steven Crowell," Toni said with mock sternness, then flung a handful of leaves at her cousin. "He didn't get a tenth of what he deserved."

"Oh, I'm not sympathizing with the rat." Susie laughed as she brushed the leaves from her hair. "My only regret is that I wasn't there to help you." She looked toward the cottage where Sara Cartlaigne was supposed to be napping. "Your 'weather report' reminds me of the old story about Aunt Sara taking a horsewhip to her intended."

"She didn't!" Toni exclaimed as she rolled over onto her stomach and propped her chin on her palms, her dark eyes bright with amusement and curiosity. "Tiny Aunt Sara wielding a horsewhip? What was the unfortunate man guilty of?"

"No one was ever certain. Or if they were, it was kept very quiet. Needless to say, the engagement ended and Aunt Sara became known as an eccentric. A label, as you well know, that has followed her to this very day."

"I don't like the word *eccentric.*" Toni frowned. "I prefer to think of her as having been a lady who knew her own mind and refused to be swayed by fads and customs she considered unworthy of her time or consideration."

Again Susie chuckled. "I suppose you would, considering the similarity in which each of you, while generations apart, handled your fiancés."

Toni grimaced at the gentle teasing, then shrugged. "I hadn't thought about that. Perhaps I'm more like her than either of us realizes."

"Antonia Elizabeth Grant! Don't be such a goose," Susie said sternly. "You're only twenty-five, an age that doesn't exactly qualify you for a lace cap and dark dresses. I can see right now that Brent and I have our work cut out for us. If we don't find you a husband during this visit, you might take it into that stubborn head of yours to become another Aunt Sara."

"Well, my goodness, Susan Louise," Toni said innocently, her dark eyes twinkling merrily. "Don't get into such a stew over the thought of your only cousin becoming an old maid."

"Old maid indeed!" Susie scoffed, her own dark eyes narrowed disapprovingly. "As a matter of fact, we'll get this little project off to a great start tomorrow evening with a nice little dinner for four at our place. You be there by six thirty, and wear something sexy."

"How about if I arrive topless, dressed in a harem veil and pants, with a large glittering gem glued to my navel?"

"You wouldn't dare!" Susie said in mock horror.

"Oh . . ." Toni sighed as though disappointed that her plan hadn't been met with more enthusiasm. "I suppose I wouldn't. But just think of it, Susie," she said with a grin. "You'd be the most talked about hostess in Natchez."

"An honor I can well do without, I assure you," Susie remarked dryly as she rolled to her knees, then stood. "I really do hate to break this up, but it's almost four thirty. My husband and son should be home any minute with their smelly catch."

"You don't sound pleased." Toni smiled as she began to walk her cousin to her car which was parked in the driveway.

"I'm not. Fishing is a passion with both of them, and they very seldom fail to return home without something to show for their efforts."

Just as they reached the car, Susie turned and looked beyond Toni's shoulder toward the two-story elegance of Cartlaigne, whose upper level and attic were visible above the trees that separated it from the cottage's property. "Looks like Aunt Sara's neighbors have returned."

Toni turned in time to see the outline of a man standing at one of the upstairs windows, staring down at the two women. "Didn't you mention that the owners were getting a divorce?" she asked.

"That was the gossip going around. Maybe they've decided to put the house on the market again." Susie shrugged. She got into the car and started the engine, then looked at Toni. "I'll be expecting you promptly at six thirty tomorrow evening—and properly clothed."

Toni laughed and waved as the small car eased down the graveled drive and out the main entrance that served both the big house and the cottage.

As she turned and made her way toward the old brick pathway that circled the cottage, she couldn't help but wonder about the man she'd seen at the window. She felt a twinge of sadness at the thought of Cartlaigne being sold again. Her ancestors, generations of them, had lived, loved, and died there. Somehow it didn't seem right for the property to be without someone to care for it.

"But the size of it," she murmured as she came to a break in the trees and stared broodingly at the imposing structure. "It boggles the mind just thinking of caring for the first floor."

With a resigned shake of her head, she continued past the rear of the cottage to one of two small, neat white structures that sat in each corner of the spacious grounds. In one building was housed a lawnmower, rakes, and other yard and garden tools. There was also food for the evil-tempered billy goat of undetermined age that Sara Cartlaigne had raised, as well as ground corn for a feisty rooster that kept the goat company.

Toni filled two small plastic pails with the concoctions that composed the daily diet of the two pets. Then she walked to the enclosure behind the building to feed the cantankerous creatures.

The goat, appropriately named Billy, was methodically gnawing away at the corner of the covered shed that afforded him protection from the cold and rain. He cast a mean-eyed glance her way as Toni hung the pails on two hooks attached to a sturdy post that supported the fence.

She bent and picked up her protection, a nice sturdy broom handle, then released the latch on the gate and entered the enclosure. The rooster, who was scratching in one deserted corner, puffed his feathers and gave every indication of attacking, only to scamper away when Toni gave a healthy swing of the broomstick.

Toni couldn't help but grin as she wondered what her friends in Richmond would say if they could see her involved in what had become a daily chore.

All such thoughts came to a halt, however, when out of the corner of her eye she caught a glimpse of Billy making his way alongside the fence in order to get a dead aim on her derriere.

She quickly dropped the pails to the ground, whipped her "club" from beneath her arm, and waved it threateningly at the cross-eyed goat. "Don't even think about it," she muttered in warning.

Billy stared at her for several seconds, then gave what Toni could have sworn was a yellow-toothed leer and swung away to feast on a piece of paper that had found its way into his domain.

"One of these days, you ornery cuss, I'm going to offer you as the main course at a barbecue," she threatened without any real malice in her voice. For as ridiculous as it seemed, there was something about Billy that reminded her of Aunt Sara.

Each of them, in their own way, could be rude and unpredictable. And, as Susie had pointed out during one of her visits, it took someone unusually determined to get along with either the goat or Aunt Sara. "But then . . . you've always been close to her, haven't you?" Susie had said to Toni.

Toni had smiled and nodded. "I've always admired her spirit. Even when I was a child—and she was an old lady then—I considered her the most fascinating person in my life. For weeks after each visit to Natchez, my mother would be ready to box my ears. For not only did I love Aunt Sara, I tried to be like her."

And now, Toni thoughtfully mused as she tipped out the first bucket of feed, *here I am, still feeling the bond, the pull of affection that exists between that tiny gray-haired old lady and me. I was hurt, and the one place in all the world I wanted to be was at Cartlaigne with Aunt Sara.*

She took a deep breath of crisp autumn air and slowly shook her head. She didn't pretend to understand the workings of fate, nor was she about to waste pointless thought and energy pondering it. She was happy and content, and at the moment that was all that mattered.

Just as she reached for the bucket containing the rooster's ground corn, Toni heard the sound of heavy footsteps coming toward her along the brick pathway. It must be Mr. Timmons, she decided. He'd spent the morning working in the yard and had probably left some of his equipment.

But when the footsteps reached the corner of the storage house, Toni could see that it definitely wasn't Mr. Timmons, the gardener. The man paused, then propped one strong arm against the shed and smiled at her.

She stared speechlessly at Christian Barr, the pail slipping from her hand and landing bottom up on the ground at her feet.

"What are you doing here?" she finally sputtered as she continued to stare disbelievingly at him.

"Now, is that any way to greet your new neighbor?" Christian asked, his dark eyes running over her jeans-clad body, then touching on the goat, the rooster, and the spilled feed.

"My neighbor?" Toni repeated incredulously. Good Lord! Was he the man she'd seen earlier at the window? "Don't tell me you've bought Cartlaigne?" The question tumbled from her lips and Christian grinned.

"Ahh . . . I can see you're still as gracious and even-tempered as I remembered. As for the house, I've leased it for six months."

Six months! Toni could see the quiet, peaceful days of her future being thrown into complete chaos. She could well imagine the grounds of Cartlaigne being overrun with his guests, the solitude shattered by the wild parties he was famous for throwing.

During her brief moments of unhappy reflection, Toni failed to notice that Christian Barr had walked around the enclosure and through the gate. The surprise that registered on her face when she turned and saw him beside her changed to something akin to horror as she watched him go down on one knee with the intention of scooping up the corn and returning it to the pail.

The events of the next few seconds seemed like a movie in slow motion. Instead of her hastily spoken "You'd better get out of here" having the desired effect upon her new neighbor, he merely paused with a double handful of grain before him and frowned up at her.

Before Toni could say more than "The goat" and point, cross-eyed Billy had somehow managed to draw a dead aim on Christian Barr and was charging, head down, for all he was worth!

The impact sent Christian sprawling amid bits of hay, straw, and goat droppings. A fine shower of ground corn settled over his large frame like the flakes of a first snow.

Once his mission was accomplished, Billy gave a triumphant bleat, shook his head back and forth a few times, then trotted back to the corner of his shelter and began to chew on his favorite piece of wood.

Toni was gripped by a paralysis that was broken only when she saw Christian Barr gingerly raise one hand to his forehead and heard the most awful flow of curse words streaming from his mouth.

She ran to him then, not sure whether to try to help him to his feet or leave him alone. She settled the dilemma by attempting to brush the corn from his head and shoulders. "Are you hurt badly?" she asked anxiously. "Can you sit up?"

Christian slowly turned his dark head and leveled such a blazing look at her that Toni withdrew the hand that was resting on his shoulder and sat back on her heels.

"Who the hell owns that goat?" he asked in a tone that could only be described as frozen fury.

"M-my aunt Sara," Toni stammered. "I'm terribly sorry. Of course I'll pay for any medical bills. Do you think you can stand up?"

"That cross-eyed bastard should be shot and his owner sued!" Christian roared, staring at the culprit.

"Now just a minute," Toni threw right back at him. "I've apologized for what happened to you and I've offered to pay your medical bills. And while I share your opinion of the goat, I don't like you talking that way about my aunt Sara." She gave him a cool smile as he pushed himself into a sitting position. "After all, you were and still are trespassing."

"Trespassing?" he roared again, his large hands busily knocking the dirt and corn from his face and hair. "In case you didn't hear me, Miss Grant, I'll repeat it. I've *leased* Cartlaigne and its grounds for six months."

"So?" Toni shrugged her shoulders dismissively.

"So," Christian began in a tone only slightly lower than before, his eyes blazing, "I don't care to be used as a battering ram by your aunt's livestock. I'm afraid the goat will have to go."

"And I think you should have the individual who drew up your contract explain to you exactly what property you leased, Mr. Barr."

Christian dropped a forearm over one updrawn knee and stared icily at her. "Now, why should I go to that trouble when I'm sure you're just dying to set me straight?"

"Very well," she briskly replied. She turned her head and nodded toward the row of trees and shrubs that ran between the big house and the cottage. "That is the property line. Which is, I might add, duly recorded in the county records. This property and that house"—she waved one hand toward the cottage and the grounds surrounding it—"are called Cartlaigne Cottage. It's owned by my aunt, Sara Cartlaigne." She turned back to the man facing her, whose temper didn't appear to be mellowing at all. "I suppose it's an easy enough mistake to make."

"How generous," Christian said acidly. "Tell me something, Antonia. . . . May I call you by your given name? I mean . . . we've shared so many intimate moments, I feel foolish addressing you as Miss Grant."

"Most of my friends call me Toni," she told him.

"Well, since I'm quite certain you don't include me in that exclusive circle, I'll stick with Antonia."

"What was your question?"

"Do you get some strange pleasure from causing pain to the men in your life? Is there some peculiar quirk in your general makeup that enjoys seeing a man maimed, bleeding, or worse?"

"Why, of course," she said innocently, striving to control her own rapidly rising temper. "I even set aside a certain time each day in which to think up new and exciting ways to declare war on the male population of the world."

"I can damn well believe it. I've met you on four different occasions. On the second one I prevented your irate fiancé from taking a swing at you. On the third I was attacked by a dog, and on the fourth I was nearly killed by a goddamn goat!"

Toni scrambled to her feet, her small body quivering with rage. "Well, maybe you wouldn't have so many problems if you didn't spend so much time poking your nose into other people's business!"

She spun around and hurried to the gate. Once she was on the other side of the barrier and the latch was firmly in place, she glared at Christian Barr. "I'll leave you to your kinsman." She waved toward the goat, who was keenly observing the antics of the two humans. "At the moment, not only do the two of you appear to have exactly the same type of personality, you also smell exactly the same!"

CHAPTER FOUR

Toni hurried through the back door of the cottage and into the "new" kitchen, which had been a sizable butler's pantry until its renovation in the early forties. Mrs. Donovan, the housekeeper, fondly referred to as Mrs. D, was putting the final touches on dinner. She turned and smiled.

"I was about to come out and check on you," the older woman told Toni. "Being two miles from town has its good points, but with it getting dark so much earlier now, I'd feel better if you would feed the animals in the morning."

"Frankly, Mrs. D, I think the animals are mean enough to look after themselves. I'm convinced that that awful old goat would be a great deal happier if he were given an endless supply of wood to eat."

"And cloth," Mrs. D added with a rueful shake of her gray head. "You dare not put anything out to air without first making sure the gate to his pen is securely fastened. By the way, I saw the lights on over at the big house. Do you think the Masons have come back?"

"No," Toni said slowly, "it's not the Masons. I ran into our new neighbor while I was looking after the animals. His name is Christian Barr."

"That sounds like a nice, romantic name." Mrs. D smiled. "Did you think to ask what line of work he's in? Is he married? How long will he be with us?"

"Unfortunately," Toni remarked dryly, "he'll be 'with us' for six months. That's how long he's leased the house. He isn't married and he's a journalist."

"Oh, my!" The housekeeper beamed. "Having such a man next door will certainly be nice. I'll have to invite him over to dinner soon."

And I'll be sure to make other plans when you do, Toni thought. "Is Aunt Sara feeling better after her nap?"

"I'm not so sure," Mrs. D replied in a concerned voice. She paused in her dinner preparations and looked at Toni. "Brent and Susie did explain about the light strokes, didn't they?" At Toni's confirming nod, Mrs. D went on. "Well, I'm no doctor, mind you, but I think she's had another one."

"Today?"

"Within the last few days. She's not as alert as she's been, and I noticed when I was dressing her for dinner that she's favoring her right arm."

"Shouldn't we call the doctor?" Toni asked, her concern apparent in her eyes.

"I did," Mrs. D calmly assured her. "But since her regular visit is in the morning, and considering how upset she gets if a fuss is made, he suggested we not say anything. We're to watch her closely. If there are any sudden changes, then of course we're to call him."

"Are you satisfied with that, Mrs. D?" Toni asked doubtfully. "I realize you've been with Aunt Sara for over thirty years and probably know her better than her family does. Do you think having the doctor out to see her would upset her?"

"Very much so, honey," the older woman said patiently. "At her age, it becomes a matter of intense pride for her to *think* she's still in control of her life. Your aunt has been blessed. Though she's not as sharp as she once was, on her good days she's amazingly alert." She patted Toni on the shoulder. "Don't worry so; she'll be fine. You scoot to your room and get dressed for dinner. It's almost six o'clock and Sara doesn't like to be kept waiting."

Toni did as she was instructed, pausing briefly at the door of the room that Aunt Sara always referred to as the sitting room. She peered in, looking for the tiny figure of her aunt, and smiled with relief when she saw that seemingly indomitable lady sitting in a large chair, her back ramrod straight. Her ebony cane was leaning against an arm of the chair and Aunt Sara was intently watching a noisy western.

Toni turned and walked to her room, the sound of bullets flying and horses pounding through *Dry Gulch Canyon* echoing in the background.

As she removed a long skirt and a blouse from the large armoire that served as a closet, she found her thoughts centering on Christian Barr. Seeing him there at Cartlaigne had been one of the biggest shocks of her life.

What can he possibly be doing in Natchez? she wondered as she undressed and stepped into the shower. She would have thought that his kind shunned quiet, sleepy rural towns for the more flamboyant life of the larger cities. In his career he'd covered civil uprisings in foreign countries and interviewed some of the highest officials in the land. What was there in Natchez to compare with that?

But it wasn't so much his professional interest that had her mind swirling. It was the man himself. He possessed a certain charisma; a smoldering sense of excitement surrounded him. Despite herself Toni had to admit that he was an unusually intriguing man.

She stepped from the shower and reached for a towel, a dark frown on her face as she wondered how best to avoid her new neighbor. Moving hurriedly, she entered her bedroom and began to dress. "I only hope he isn't seriously injured from his bout with that damn goat," she muttered as she donned fresh underwear, then slipped into the skirt and blouse she'd laid out earlier. "On second thought," she said with an evil grimace, "it would be a novel experience to see the infamous Mr. Barr pitted against Aunt Sara. There's no doubt in my mind who the winner would be."

With genuine amusement, Toni wondered if her aunt could still be persuaded to make use of her old twelve-gauge shotgun, an item that in years gone by had done a great deal to enhance the old woman's reputation as an eccentric.

She was still smiling at the thought of a confrontation between her aunt and their new neighbor when she heard the tiny bell Aunt Sara kept on the table beside her chair. That sharp, tinkling sound meant that dinner would begin in five minutes. It also meant that family and guests would also present themselves in what their hostess considered suitable attire; jackets and ties for the men, dresses—preferably long ones—for the women.

When Toni reached the door of the sitting room, she met Aunt Sara, leaning heavily on her cane, with Mrs. D close but not actually touching the older woman.

Sara Cartlaigne, as tiny as her niece, was dressed in a long navy-blue velvet dress. Her snowy white hair was worn up in a smooth coronet style that hadn't changed for as long as Toni could remember. And though her face bore the lines of age, the years had been kind. Her skin was soft and her eyes were bright and sparkling.

"I'm sorry to have kept you waiting," Toni said with a smile as she leaned over and kissed a soft cheek. "Billy was rather testy when I went to feed him."

"Don't apologize, Antonia," Sara briskly shushed her niece. "Having you in this old house has done wonders for Mrs. D and me. Being a few minutes late isn't a crime." She smiled. "Take my arm, child. I'm not as steady on my feet as I once was."

Toni did as she was told, careful to maintain a cheerful expression. She kept up a steady stream of chatter and felt especially grateful to hear her aunt laugh. Asking for someone's arm and admitting to any sort of physical weakness wasn't Aunt Sara's style.

Once they entered the dining room and were seated at the huge old mahogany table, Sara questioned Toni at length regarding Billy, the work Mr. Timmons had done in the yard earlier in the day, and Susie's visit.

Toni painted a comical picture of the aging goat, but was careful to leave out any mention of their newest neighbor's encounter with the family pet. She dutifully recounted exactly where Mr. Timmons had planted the spring bulbs and explained that the leaves from the large oaks were being used as mulch in the flower beds.

"Susie has invited me to her house for dinner tomorrow evening. I think she has it in her mind to find a husband for me."

"Susie's a sweet girl and I'm fond of her, but she's something of a featherhead," Sara said bluntly. "She reminds me of my older sister Caroline. She was always running about, trying to arrange other people's lives."

Toni threw Mrs. D an amused glance. "Well, I can't vouch for Aunt Caroline, but Susie doesn't mean to interfere. In fact, I'm looking forward to seeing what sort of man she thinks will suit me. Brent's taken, so that narrows the field considerably, don't you agree?"

"I do." Toni's spritelike relative smiled. "But a man as easygoing as Brent would never do for you, Antonia. You need a man with spirit, one who's capable of matching that temper of yours. You're a Cartlaigne, my dear, from the top of your head to the tips of your toes. We're not known for our meek, submissive ways. In some ways it's a blessing, in others it's a curse."

"So far I've found it to be the latter." Toni sighed as she thought back to the abrupt manner in which she'd terminated her engagement to Steven. Perhaps she'd been too hasty in her decision.

"One must never look back, Antonia. Only fools waste their time crying over what might have been. Consider yourself lucky to have gotten out of an unfortunate situation and concentrate on the future," Sara lectured. "But not too quickly," she added with a smile. "I like having you here. Besides, this place will be yours at my death. You're the last Cartlaigne female."

"Aunt Sara . . . please," Toni said, trying in vain

to stop her. "I don't want to even think of such a thing happening."

"But you must think about it, and be prepared to accept your responsibility. This cottage is all that's left to represent the efforts and love of generations of your ancestors. It'll be up to you to see that it's kept up."

Toni fidgeted uncomfortably beneath her aunt's intense gaze. She could have hugged Mrs. D, who chose that moment to speak, then could just as easily have taped shut the dear woman's mouth as she listened to the housekeeper talking about there being someone next door.

This news seemed to please Aunt Sara, who expressed a definite dislike for "that last young man and his flighty wife."

After dinner was over, Toni saw her aunt to her chair in the sitting room while the housekeeper cleared the table.

Once she had Aunt Sara seated in the comfortable chair, Toni was careful to tuck the warm folds of an afghan about her knees and ankles. "Now," she said with a smile as she bent and kissed one softly lined cheek, "that should keep you snug and warm. Are you ready for your sherry?"

"I suppose so, but only half a glass, Antonia," her aunt instructed. "It relaxes me and makes me sleepy."

"That's what it's supposed to do." Toni chuckled as she walked over to a delicately carved rosewood table on which sat a tray holding glasses, as well as a decanter each of sherry, bourbon, and Scotch. She was careful to pour only the requested amount of sherry, thinking, rather amusedly, what a comedown it was for her aunt. Until about four years ago Sara Cartlaigne's after-dinner toddy had been a neat three fingers of bourbon.

Toni carried the small, stemmed glass over to her aunt, an apologetic expression on her face. "I realize you would rather have the bourbon and I wish I could give it to you."

"That's one of the many things about you that I love, Antonia." Sara smiled conspiratorially. "You understand me. Your mother—God rest her soul—and Susie have always thought of me as being one step from AA."

"Nonsense," said Toni. "I'd much rather see you enjoying your toddy than having to take some sort of tranquilizer."

The next hour was spent as each evening after dinner had been since Toni's arrival in Natchez. Sara entertained her niece with lively stories of the past. And if Toni had heard the stories numerous times and knew them by heart, she never let on. For to her, her great-aunt was special, and if the small amount of time Aunt Sara spent in reliving her past made her happy, then Toni considered it the most important part of her day.

By the time Mrs. D joined them, however, Aunt Sara was attempting to hide her yawns behind the lace-trimmed handkerchief she always kept handy. Toni and the housekeeper exchanged knowing glances as the stories became slightly less coherent and the voice a little more halting.

When the tiny head finally began to nod, Mrs. D suggested that it was getting late. Aunt Sara immediately agreed. "I think you should go to bed as well, Antonia," she told her niece. "Late nights can take the bloom out of a young girl's cheeks."

Toni smothered her amusement at this advice as she leaned forward for the peck on her cheek that her aunt doled out nightly. "I won't be far behind you," Toni hedged, then stepped aside and watched the housekeeper guide her charge from the room.

As she turned back to the softly glowing coals of the small fire, Toni heard the commanding sound of the grandfather clock in the hallway strike nine times. Bloom in her cheeks or not, there was no way she could go to bed at such an early hour.

She glanced around the high-ceilinged room at the priceless antique furnishings. And though she had a deep sense of love and pride in her surroundings, Toni found herself feeling anxious for the first time since her arrival at Cartlaigne Cottage.

It didn't take her long to pinpoint the source of her uneasiness. It was in the shape and form of the nasty man who had moved next door . . . Christian Barr.

She sat on the sofa and stared moodily at the fire, conjuring up all sorts of unflattering pictures of her new neighbor. Her favorite showed him as an aging Lothario, leering lasciviously at each young girl he encountered.

I wonder how old he really is? she thought. For in all she'd read and heard about him, his age hadn't been mentioned. At least she couldn't remember if it had. *Perhaps he's much younger than he looks,* she thought. Men who lived the kind of life Christian Barr was supposed to lead would surely age prematurely, she concluded smugly.

Toni shifted restlessly, annoyed with herself for allowing that man to dominate her thoughts. Hadn't she suffered the ultimate humiliation at Steven's hands?

And wasn't Steven a small-time version of Christian Barr?

"Of course he is," she muttered out loud. But the hurt and the anger were still there, still simmering behind the façade of happiness and well-being she presented to the public.

It was easy to sit back and say she'd been lucky to find out about Steven when she had. But as she looked back on that evening when she discovered how little her love had meant to him, Toni knew it would be a long time before she would truly get over the pain.

The experience had left her wondering if she could ever really trust a man again. She *had* trusted Steven. She'd thought his love as unshakable as a mountain. And she'd never been more completely wrong in her life.

Perhaps part of the blame was hers, Toni thought. Prior to the accident her relationship with Steven had been fairly casual. She hadn't bothered to delve into his emotional makeup because she hadn't been looking for a husband. She was young, happy with her life and the direction in which her career was headed.

After the accident, however, she had wanted someone to take care of her, someone strong and kind and understanding. Steven had seemed to offer all the protection she was looking for.

She wondered if he had been aware of her needs and had taken advantage of them for some reason of his own. His parents had been thrilled at the news of their engagement. Was it possible that they'd been urging him to get married and settle down? If so, what better choice for a wife than one without any family to interfere.

She also recalled his cutting remark during that

stormy exchange on her last day at work. He'd said, in effect, that being Mrs. Steven Crowell should make up for any embarrassment she might have suffered from his seeing Lea Simmons.

"The pompous ass!" Toni softly exclaimed just as the telephone sounded. The harsh ringing seemed out of place, and after her initial start at the noise, she hurried to answer.

Her quiet "Hello?" was spoken rather breathlessly, considering that she had to run all the way to the kitchen and the only phone her aunt would allow in the house.

"Antonia?" a deep voice boomed in her ear. "This is Christian Barr. Thanks to that damn goat, I've got a roaring headache. I need to see a doctor, but I think it would be wise if someone drove me. Would it be asking too much of you to perform that small neighborly task?"

The combination of hearing his voice and the fact that he was ill threw Toni into a panic. Having decided that he was a thoroughly detestable man, she could just see him causing all sorts of trouble for Aunt Sara.

"I'll be right over," she said hastily.

After replacing the receiver, she stood undecided in the middle of the kitchen. If she were to go in and tell Mrs. D where she was going, Aunt Sara would have to be filled in on all the details. And knowing her aunt as she did, Toni could well imagine the confusion that that would bring about. She finally settled on leaving the housekeeper a note taped to the front of the fridge.

After that small matter was taken care of, she raced to her room where she exchanged the skirt and blouse she was wearing for a pair of jeans and a sweater. She grabbed a jacket and her purse, then retraced her steps to the kitchen and out the back door.

As she hurried along the path that ran from the cottage and through the barrier of shrubs and trees to the big house, the only lights Toni could see were the ones in the rooms to the rear. So instead of going around to the imposing front entrance, she made her way up the wide cypress steps of the side gallery to a door that she remembered as opening into a downstairs sitting room.

Just as she reached up to grasp the heavy knocker, the door was wrenched open and a scowling Christian reached for her arm.

"It's about time," he rasped in a rough voice as he pulled her inside, then slammed the door.

"I did have to leave a note for the housekeeper," Toni remarked in a stiff voice, then pulled her arm from his grasp. As she spoke she saw the ugly raised lump over his right eye. "That . . . that looks painful," she said in a kinder tone.

"Of course it's painful," Christian said tightly. "That damned goat knocked me into a steel water pipe."

Toni's eyes quickly traversed the length and breadth of her patient, her lips tightening with resignation as she prepared herself for a long and trying evening. Christian was dressed in jeans and a dark pullover and looked mean enough to go bear hunting with a switch.

"Well?" he demanded in a near roar. "Are you going to stare at me all night or are you going to take me to see a doctor?"

Toni met his glaring blue eyes with her own dark

smoldering ones. "I doubt you'll die from being butted in the rear by a goat."

"In case you haven't noticed, it's my head and not my rear that needs attention," Christian said icily.

"Sorry." Toni sighed. "You're acting like such an ass, I got the two confused." She dropped her purse onto a table beside the door, then stepped around him. "Where is the phone?"

"On that desk." Christian nodded toward a massive, heavily carved piece of furniture in one corner of the enormous room, then gave a sharp gasp. Toni swung back around in time to see him holding an unsteady hand to his head.

Oh, Lord! she thought. *He really is in pain.* Momentarily forgetting her distaste for the man, and the fact that his presence was as welcome as the plague, she caught him by one arm and urged him toward a chair.

"Please sit down while I call Brent."

"Who the hell is Brent?"

"My cousin Susie's husband. He's a doctor."

"Well, at least the two of you aren't related by blood." Christian scowled. "I can only hope he hasn't been around you long enough for your disaster-prone ways to have rubbed off on him."

"If you're that concerned," Toni sweetly countered, "I can always go back to my aunt's and let you fend for yourself." She stood directly in front of him, one hand on her hip as she narrowly eyed him. "What's it to be?"

Christian allowed his dark head to drop back against the chair and closed his eyes. "Call your damn cousin. If he kills me, then at least I'll be out of my misery."

"I should be so lucky," Toni muttered to herself as she turned and walked toward the phone.

"I heard that, Antonia."

"Good for you, Christian," she threw over her shoulder, unperturbed. "At least Billy left your eardrums intact."

Toni dialed her cousin's number, and after a brief conversation Brent agreed to meet them at the emergency room.

The drive to the hospital got under way only after another altercation regarding transportation.

"I prefer to go in my own car," Toni informed Christian as she stared at his black Lincoln. It looked as long as a hearse and would be the very devil to park. "As you can see, it's foggy and I'd really rather not be driving a strange car under these conditions."

"Do you still have the Subaru you were driving in Virginia?" he asked.

"Yes."

"Then we'll take mine," he replied in such a manner as to lead Toni to believe he wouldn't change his mind. "My head already feels as though it's been split in half. I have no intention of being jostled to death in that tin can of yours."

Toni refrained from commenting, although she thought that a good brain scrambling might do wonders for his personality.

Fortunately Christian wasn't one of those people who looked for instant death at every curve or expected a spook to jump from behind every tree. And even on the two or three occasions when Toni almost sent him sailing through the windshield, due to the extreme sensitivity of the brakes on the Lincoln, there was no bark of reproval from him.

By the time she'd completed the drive and was parking at the emergency entrance of the hospital, Toni found herself honestly feeling sorry for the large, silent man beside her.

CHAPTER FIVE

Without thinking, Toni removed the keys from the ignition and handed them to Christian. "You wait here while I get someone with a wheelchair."

"I have a headache, Antonia," he said with a frown. "There's nothing wrong with my legs."

"Oh, but—" she started, then stopped. Christian already had his door open and was climbing out. Toni hurried around the car to his side and slipped a sustaining arm around his waist. "Lean your weight on me," she instructed him, a worried frown on her face.

And for the first time since before Billy's attack in the goat pen, Toni heard Christian laugh. She threw a startled glance up at him, wondering if he'd suffered more serious damage than she'd first imagined.

Without thinking, she raised her left hand and wiggled it before his face. "Are you having trouble focusing, Christian?" *Oh, my God!* she thought frantically. *I can see it now. "Noted Journalist Sues 96-Year-Old Woman over Goat."*

"Can you see my hand?" she asked anxiously. "Count my fingers."

Christian dutifully counted off the wiggling digits beneath his nose, still wearing such a silly grin that Toni was convinced he was fast becoming a basket case. "Does that make you happy?" he asked.

Toni regarded him for several seconds, indecision plainly written in her face. "I suppose so," she murmured, then tightened her arm around his waist and urged him forward. "Let's get you inside so Brent can take a look at you."

Instead of doddering along like someone in his condition was supposed to, Christian looped one long arm across her shoulders and proceeded to the entrance as though they were out for a late evening stroll. Toni was about to point out that there was no need for him to hold her so tightly when Brent appeared at the door.

"Ah . . . here you are." Brent smiled, relieving Toni of her burden. "I was about to head out your way and see if you'd had car trouble."

"Sorry," she said tightly as she moved away from Christian's side, "but we didn't get started as soon as I thought we should."

She introduced the two men, then stood back and watched them disappear down a corridor and into an examining room.

As she waited for Brent to examine Christian, Toni alternated between sitting and pacing. She also tried to push to the back of her mind the memory of Christian's arm around her shoulder and the scent of his after-shave, which still lingered on the sleeve of her jacket.

Don't be silly, she lectured herself as she paced. *It's*

perfectly normal to feel some small attraction for the man, darn it. But don't even let yourself think beyond that point. Just hope that whatever business brought him to Natchez can be completed well ahead of schedule, and that he'll soon be on his way.

Sometime later she was standing, staring out the window at the parking lot, when she heard the sound of familiar voices. She turned and saw Brent and Christian, chatting away like long-lost friends. Toni went forward to meet them, her eyes searching the face of the tall figure beside her cousin for some indication of how severely he was injured. Seeing nothing but a pair of lazy blue eyes sweeping her from head to foot, Toni looked back at Brent.

"Well? Will he live?" she asked, and was immediately ashamed of how harsh the question sounded. But damn it! The supposed patient had no business ogling her.

If Brent was aware of her nervousness, he didn't show it. He clapped Christian on the shoulder and grinned. "All this fellow needs is a couple of days' rest. There is a concussion, but it's very slight. The shot I gave him might make him a little light-headed, so be sure and see that he's settled for the night before you leave him. I told him I was sure you and Mrs. D would be happy to look after him, since there's no one at Cartlaigne to do it."

"Of course," Toni said faintly. She was relieved that the injury wasn't more serious, but she wasn't looking forward to playing nurse to Christian Barr.

With her "duties" for the next few days having been outlined for her, Toni had no choice but to stand by and listen as Brent and Christian discussed a common interest, their passion for fishing!

After being forced to listen to outlandish fish stories for several minutes as Brent eagerly acquainted Christian with each and every body of water within a fifty-mile radius of the city, Toni decided she'd had enough.

"Since you guys seem to have so much to talk about, why don't I run along and let you continue this interesting conversation?" She smiled innocently at each of them, then concentrated on Christian. "I'm sure Brent won't mind driving you out to Cartlaigne."

But Christian had no intention of letting her off the hook so easily. With practiced ease, he brought the conversation to a halt, apologized to Brent for disturbing him at such a late hour, and was escorting Toni to the car before she had time to do more than give a brief wave of good-bye to her cousin.

"Are you regretting your decision already?" he asked as they began the drive back to Cartlaigne.

Without looking directly at him, Toni could tell that he was very relaxed and that his gaze hadn't left her since they'd gotten into the car.

"What decision is that?" she asked casually, forcing herself to concentrate on her driving rather than the disturbing presence of the man beside her.

"The one you made this afternoon, when you so graciously asked me to let you know if there were any . . . er . . . repercussions from my encounter with your aunt's goat," he smoothly replied.

"Of course not," Toni said. "After all, you were injured on our property, so it's only fair that we take full responsibility."

"Does that include round-the-clock nursing?" Christian asked.

Toni shot him a quick, mean look. "Don't press

your luck, Christian. But in case that becomes necessary, Mrs. D has a sister who does private duty."

"Who the hell is Mrs. D? That's the second time I've heard her name mentioned this evening."

"My aunt's housekeeper. She's in her early sixties, and her sister is a couple of years older." Toni threw him a wicked grin. "So *please* don't worry for a single minute about competent care. Mrs. Henderson is very efficient."

"I just bet she is," he remarked acidly. "But I think, rather than bother Mrs. Henderson, I'd prefer a younger woman. Perhaps one with dark hair and eyes. A woman who possessess a certain propensity for making things happen. Do you have any idea where I might find such a person?"

Toni kept her eyes glued to the road and the sharp curve they were approaching. But the minute they were on a straight stretch of highway, she was quick to defend herself.

"I didn't invite you into the goat's pen," she said crossly. "As usual, you were poking your nose where it didn't belong."

"Oh?" Christian asked softly. "Is that what I was doing the morning I stopped your fiancé from belting you?"

"Ex-fiancé," Toni corrected spiritedly. "And I prefer to think he was merely bluffing."

"Then that shows how little you know about Steven Crowell. Believe me, honey, he hadn't drawn back his hand to caress your cheek," he bluntly reminded her.

"Shall we drop the subject? I find it difficult to believe you came all this way to discuss my relationship with Steven."

"That's partly true. But what would you say if I

were to tell you that I chose Natchez because I knew you would be here?"

"I think I'd probably ask how you knew my travel plans," Toni replied with outward calm. Inwardly she was seething. Just who the hell did he think he was? And how dare he assume that, for whatever real reason there was behind his appearance next door, she would be impressed by such a ridiculous statement as he'd just made.

"That's simple, Antonia," he said unhesitatingly. "Your friend Connie was eager to fill me in on all the details regarding your family and your affection for your aunt. Once she told me the names of the present owners of Cartlaigne, and I realized they were old friends of mine who own a chain of newspapers, leasing the house became quite simple."

"Sounds as though Connie was as informative as an encyclopedia," Toni said, frowning.

"Only because I told her that I wanted to get to know you better," Christian said pleasantly. "I find I'm intrigued by the excitement that seems to surround you," he added.

And in spite of herself, Toni grinned. "Are you certain you're physically up to 'getting to know me better?' " she asked as they approached the entrance to Cartlaigne. "I mean, look at what's happened so far. You were almost involved in a brawl, you *were* attacked by a dog—a small one, but nevertheless a dog—and you suffered a slight concussion at the hands—or rather head—of my aunt's goat."

She parked the car at the side entrance, switched off the ignition, then turned her head and stared intently at him. "If I were you, Christian, I do believe I'd reconsider. For a man of your age and reputation, not to mention your obvious lack of stamina, a really dedicated pursuit of me might prove fatal."

In the dim lighting of the confined space, Christian met the rather amused and, at the same time, derisive glint in Toni's eyes with his own determined gaze. He'd known since the first moment he saw her that he *would* get to know her better.

Admittedly, the events that followed hadn't exactly gone as he'd first planned. Toni's departure from Richmond had come as a complete surprise to him. But he had already decided to take six months or so off to think about changes in his career, and he hadn't had any definite travel plans in mind, so choosing Natchez had been an easy enough thing to do.

That decision had been helped along by taking Connie to dinner. During the course of the evening Christian had learned the reason for Toni's breakup with Steven Crowell and that she had relatives in Natchez. When Connie, eager to acquaint him with each tiny scrap of information regarding Toni, mentioned that the present owner of Cartlaigne was the son of a publishing tycoon and that the house was vacant, Christian took care of the matter from that point on.

Now here he was, sitting next to a pixie-eyed minx who'd stayed in his thoughts for days. To add insult to injury, there was about as much welcome reflected in her voice and in the dark pools of her eyes as he imagined her ancestors felt when the Yankees had invaded Cartlaigne over a hundred years ago.

Not only was she not overjoyed to see him, she'd actually had the nerve to cast aspersions upon him, his manhood, and the reputation to which he'd devoted so much time and effort.

It was a slight fidgeting from his pint-size chauffeur

that caused Christian to break the tense silence. "Don't let my past 'failings' worry you, Antonia." He smiled thinly. "When I decide to pursue a lady, I always make a point of fortifying myself with all sorts of vitamins. I have to consider my age, you see. My companions are never disappointed, and neither will you be."

"You're ridiculous," Toni said flatly, unable to believe the incredible gall of the man.

"No." Christian sighed. "At the moment I'm just injured. Not only is my head pounding like crazy, but that shot is beginning to make me feel a little dizzy."

Toni wanted desperately to run to the safety of the cottage, but she knew she ought to see Christian safely inside his own place.

"Can you walk or do you need me to help you?" she finally asked after several seconds of soul-searching.

Christian shrugged. "If you'll lend me a hand, I would appreciate it."

Telling herself that it was the shot that caused Christian to talk the way he did, Toni opened the door and hurried around to the passenger side to assist him.

"Just slip an arm across my shoulders," she told him as she caught him tight around the waist and tried to compensate for the almost comical disparity in their heights. "Walk slowly, and please be careful of the steps," she cautioned. "They'll be slippery as glass from the dew."

"You're such a tiny thing," he said, smiling down at her. "Are you sure you can get me up to the porch?" With that question, his arm about her shoulders tightened and Toni found herself glued to his side.

His touch seemed to burn right through her clothes and sear her skin from shoulder to thigh. At her attempt to lessen the body contact, Christian swayed dangerously, and Toni found herself clutching him and holding on for dear life.

"I should have called Brent out here," she said worriedly after getting the two of them standing upright again and lined up with the wide steps. "That shot made you as drunk as a Bourbon Street bum."

"But it's gotten you in my arms . . . or rather me in yours, hasn't it?" He grinned crookedly. Before Toni could do more than stare helplessly up at him, he dipped his head and delivered a loud, smacking kiss that landed on the side of her nose. "Oops." He chortled. "My vitamins are working, but my aim is off."

"Cute," Toni remarked disgustedly as she led, pushed, and tugged him toward the porch and up the steps. "Other people are sitting by a cozy fire reading a good book or watching their favorite TV show. Me? I'm having to deal with a drunken maniac who can't hit his behind with both hands, but who's still trying to retain the crown of Mr. Playboy!"

"Tsk, tsk." Christian grinned wickedly and wagged a long, square-tipped finger beneath her nose. "Just because ol' Steven didn't come through for you doesn't mean all men are duds."

"I can't tell you how reassuring that bit of information is, Christian. It really warms my heart." Toni glared at him. She maneuvered him so that he was standing with his back to the wall beside the door, then placed a palm flat against his chest with the terse order to "Stay put." She held out her other hand. "I need the key."

"Forget the damn key," he muttered as he reached out with both arms and pulled her to him. "I want to kiss you."

Toni thoughtfully nibbled at one corner of her bottom lip as she stared up at him. The entire situation was ridiculous and had become rather comical. For the life of her, she found herself unable to stay mad at him. "Don't you ever give up?" she asked, struggling to keep from laughing.

"Never!" he declared as emphatically as his befuddled mind would allow him. "We Barr men are famous for our virility, determination, and the ability to pick a pretty lass with a trim . . . er . . . ankle."

"A trim ankle?" she squeaked incredulously, then burst out laughing. "You sound like a not so very good pirate."

"I'm a descendant of a varied and exciting line," he solemnly declared.

"Oh, I'm sure you must be," Toni said with a nod. "But before you catch pneumonia and end such an illustrious line, don't you think we should get you inside and to bed."

"Not without a kiss."

"You've already tried and failed."

"You weren't standing still. It was like trying to kiss a damned bobbing target."

"Getting excited isn't what you need at the moment."

"I'll risk it." He smiled lazily and Toni caught the flash of white teeth as his head swooped downward and his mouth caught hers.

She was afraid to fight him, she told herself as she felt his lips against hers. They could easily wind up in a tangled heap on the floor. But after only a moment of the gentle teasing and tasting of his tongue as it sought entrance to the warm darkness of her mouth, she found she didn't want to fight him.

He was gentle but demanding, and she felt herself responding easily and with a depth of emotion that surprised her. There was nothing hurried or frantic as his tongue entered her mouth, searching, probing, and awakening slumbering desires within her.

Toni felt the blood coursing in her veins with a swiftness she'd never known with Steven. This wasn't some tepid sort of pleasure she was feeling, but a wild, rushing torrent of excitement raging through her.

Christian's hands began to glide over her shoulders and back, then they eased down until they rested on her hips and pressed them tightly against his thighs. At that moment Toni knew she had to collect her scattered thoughts and restore some semblance of calm to the situation.

Sensing her withdrawal, Christian raised his dark head and stared down at her. And though the darkness prevented Toni from seeing the expression revealed in his blue eyes, the huskiness of his voice let her know that she wasn't the only one left breathless by the kiss.

"You, Antonia Grant, are a very sexy lady," he rasped, his breath fanning her heated cheeks. "I can't possibly imagine what made Steven Crowell look for greener pastures."

Toni smiled. "One man's pleasure . . . another man's poison?" She stepped back and held out a slightly unsteady hand. "Your key please."

Once inside, where the table lamps cast a sobering glow of normalcy over everything, Toni found herself not wanting to meet the bold gaze that followed her about the room. At Christian's nod of agreement, she got a pillow and blanket from the king-size bed in the downstairs bedroom and placed them on the sofa.

"Are you sure you'd rather sleep here than in the bed?" she asked. She finally turned to look at him and felt the same powerful attraction that had nearly been her undoing on the porch. *Stop it!* she silently argued against the inexplicable pull she felt toward this man. *At the moment he's everything you don't need. If it's an affair you want, then for heaven's sake find some kind, uncomplicated man who will take only what you want to give. Any sort of relationship with Christian Barr would be a fight to the bitter end.*

"I don't like sleeping alone in a bed," he said without the slightest embarrassment, then chuckled at the rush of color that stained Toni's cheeks.

She sighed, then walked over and picked up her purse. "The shot seems to be wearing off. Your eyes are clear again and you're back to being your usual obnoxious self."

"That's interesting," Christian remarked as he stepped in front of her and neatly blocked her path. "I didn't get up enough nerve to kiss you until the shot addled my brain." He reached out and lightly traced the outline of her lips with one finger. "Are you implying that you prefer me in a more amorous mood?"

"I don't prefer you in any mood," she returned with as much spirit as she could muster. Lying wasn't one of her strong suits and, more importantly, Christian knew it.

"Your nose is going to grow." He grinned. "Stay with me for a while. Let's get some brandy, sit on that soft rug in front of the fireplace and watch the fire."

Toni started to say she didn't want to, but decided against it. The idea was very appealing but unacceptable. "I can't."

"Are you afraid?"

"I think *cautious* or *wary* would be a better choice of words."

"Then you aren't as indifferent to me as you would have me believe, are you?"

Toni shrugged. "I'm a healthy, normal woman and you're an attractive man. That's as far as I'm willing to go."

"Well, I hate to disturb the peaceful ebb and flow of your life, honey, but I hardly see how we can live next door to each other for six months and remain polite strangers."

"It's possible."

"But not very likely, Antonia," Christian said flatly.

"Do you really mean to stay for six months?" she asked, hoping against hope that he'd say he would be gone within a week or two.

"I'm afraid it's six months, Antonia," he said, the twinkle in his eyes belying the somberness of his voice. "I figure that should give us time enough to get to know each other. I usually don't go in for longer relationships with women, but with you, I think I can be persuaded to change my routine."

Toni's expression never altered. In spite of the outright fury welling up within her, she managed to keep a calm, unruffled look about her. "I appreciate your consideration, Christian. It does something for a gal's morale to be told she's next in line as 'mistress of the month' for someone as infamous as you. However, you'll have to clear all the minor details with my cousin Susie. She's become my social secretary in hopes of marrying me off within the next few months."

She stepped around him and marched to the door. "Have a good night," she threw over her shoulder as she exited the room, then slammed the door behind her.

"Relationship indeed! An affair is more like it!" Toni muttered angrily to herself as she stalked along the path between the two houses. "Not very likely, Mr. Christian Barr."

Surely somewhere among the list of available men she was certain Susie held in eager readiness, there would be at least one individual compatible enough for her to pretend an interest in.

There had to be. For not only did she resent Christian Barr's sweeping assumption that she would drop everything and hop into his bed, but Toni had found, during those few minutes in his arms, that it might be a remarkably nice place to be.

CHAPTER SIX

Sleep was a long time coming after Toni eventually got to bed. For no matter how hard she tried, all she could think about was Christian Barr. It was as though the scent and taste of him had permeated her senses and nothing she did could erase the floating picture of his face each time she closed her eyes.

The last clear thought she had before dropping off to sleep was her hope that Mrs. D would agree to look after their new neighbor. Toni knew she would be more than willing to do any number of Mrs. D's household chores in order to be spared such an uncomfortable task.

Bright and early the next morning an apprehensive Toni was in the kitchen, explaining to the housekeeper in detail what had happened the evening before.

"You mean you actually know this Christian Barr?" Mrs. D asked, her eyes dancing merrily as she listened.

They were sitting at the sturdy work table, enjoying their first cup of coffee.

"I met him a couple of days before I left Richmond," Toni hedged. "He has a terrible reputation, Mrs. D, which I think he enjoys to the hilt."

"How exciting!" The older woman sighed. "I don't think I've ever met a man such as you've described."

"And you really want to?" Toni asked, surprised. Somehow the idea of the steady, trustworthy Mrs. D going into raptures over the thought of meeting Christian Barr seemed a bit absurd.

"Well, of course I do," she stoutly declared. "At my age all a woman has are her memories and an occasional fantasy. My husband was a good man, and I loved him dearly, but he was about as romantic as a post. So I figure any man who has such a damning reputation has to have some romance in him."

"Oh, I'm sure he's loaded with romance." Toni grinned ruefully. "What he's lacking, however, seems to be staying power."

"When he meets the right woman he'll have no trouble at all settling down," Mrs. D offered as though an expert on the subject. "Reformed rakes always make the best husbands."

"Really?" Toni asked skeptically. The thought of Christian Barr living a life of domestic bliss certainly didn't ring true to her. She saw him more as a temporary lover, a fascinating, exciting man who might give a woman a few weeks of intense happiness but then disappear, leaving her to become yet another "former" friend of his.

"As a matter of fact, I think you're the type of woman that could make a man like your Mr. Barr decide to put an end to his bachelor ways."

"Really, Mrs. D," Toni protested, her heart skipping a beat at the thought. "Believe me when I say I've had enough of men with his particular problem. Of course, that's not to say he isn't an exciting man. But who wants to live in a continuous supercharged state? Human nature being what it is, don't you think we also need the valleys as well as the peaks in life?"

"I'll reserve judgment on that until I've met our neighbor," the housekeeper answered with a smile.

"Fair enough," Toni conceded. "So, since you're willing to take care of him, make me a list of the things I can do for you."

"Well . . ." The older woman thought for a moment. "There really isn't that much to do, honey, what with the cleaning woman coming in three days a week. Your aunt is very picky about her food, so you really shouldn't try to do any of the cooking. Let's just play it by ear. If I find myself in a tight spot, I'll yell. Otherwise, don't let this little upheaval bother you."

Upheaval was hardly the word for Christian's arrival next door, Toni thought later, as she made her bed, tidied her room, then dressed. She likened his appearance more to a tornado invading a quiet, sleepy little town, throwing everything and everyone into a giant uproar.

That's not wholly true and you know it, she told herself. *He's merely a reminder—a huge reminder—of what happened between you and Steven.*

She'd come to Natchez to forget about her broken engagement, to allow her mind the same period of healing that her body had required after the accident. But with Christian around to constantly remind her, as he'd done the evening before, and to admit so bluntly that a relationship was uppermost in his mind, she knew her tranquil days were at an end.

Toni was wise enough to know that Christian wasn't

interested in halfway measures any more than he cared about a permanent relationship. She could never keep things casual with him, never hope to be just friends or neighbors. His interests were wholly centered on brief physical encounters.

Ordinarily she would have listened to his outrageous comments, laughed them off, refused, and gone on her way. But at the moment she was still smarting from Steven's rejection. Regardless of the fact that his infidelity had been conducted on the sly, and that he had always intended to marry her, his actions had left Toni with a feeling of inadequacy.

A frustrated sigh rushed past her lips. There was no need to go over and over the same thoughts that had plagued her for days. As Sara Cartlaigne had remarked, nothing was gained by looking back.

The kitchen was a veritable haven of aromas. Bacon, coffee, and blueberry muffins tantalized her senses as Toni entered the room for the second time that morning.

"Don't tell me you're going to resort to the most obvious inducement of plying our neighbor with food?" she asked as she reached around Mrs. D and filched a warm muffin.

"Why not?" The housekeeper smiled. "It'll be nice having a man to cook for. You and your aunt aren't hearty eaters."

Toni merely shrugged, then asked about her aunt's appointment with the doctor.

"It's at ten thirty. I'll take her in unless you'd rather do it."

"Since you know more about her medication and the way she likes things done, Mrs. D, it's probably best if you go with her."

"I think so," Mrs. D agreed. "She hates having the slightest change made in her routine. I also want to talk to him about these light strokes she's been having. If you'd like, why not drop by his office later and talk with him."

"Isn't he in the same clinic that Brent's associated with?" Toni asked.

"Yes, he is."

"Then I'm sure Susie will be able to fill me in on any change when I see her this evening." Toni glanced at the tray that held her aunt's breakfast. "Would you like me to take this in?"

"That might cheer her up. She slept later than usual this morning and doesn't seem to be herself. I thought I'd let her rest until it was time to get her dressed for her appointment."

When Toni entered the darkened bedroom, there wasn't the slightest movement from the small form beneath the covers. She placed the tray carefully on the round table beside the bed, then turned and stared intently at her aunt.

For a moment her heart seemed to jump up into her throat as she failed to detect any rise and fall of the tiny, frail woman's chest. Toni reached out and took one thin hand in her own warm grasp.

"Aunt Sara?" she said urgently. "Aunt Sara?"

There was the barest pressure against Toni's hand, and the slow turning of a small white head. Eyes clouded with age opened and looked up at her.

"Ellen," her aunt said clearly. "Why on earth are you hovering over me like that? Has Papa found out about you meeting that Donaldson boy?"

"It's Antonia, Aunt Sara. I've brought you some coffee and juice," Toni said softly. She reached for another fluffy pillow. "Let me put this pillow behind your shoulders. We can talk while you sip your coffee."

This seemed to please Sara, and in nothing flat, Toni had her reclining against the pillows with the tray across her lap.

Toni sat on the edge of the bed and smiled lovingly at her aunt. "Did you sleep well?"

"Of course I did, silly. Was Papa upset with you?"

There was no point in trying to correct her, Toni decided, so she answered in kind. "At first he was very angry. But he's calmed down now. Don't you think it's time for you to get up and start getting dressed?"

"Oh, I suppose so," Sara answered disgustedly. "You know, I really don't care for lawn parties. All you get are grass stains on the hems of your dresses and petticoats, and a sunburn on your nose. Then there's that horrible punch the Hamiltons serve. It tastes like vinegar."

"Maybe it will rain today and you won't have to attend," Toni said calmly. This was the second or third time since her arrival that she'd seen her aunt become completely lost in the past. It wasn't pleasant witnessing someone you loved losing their grip on reality. Yet Toni knew this was to be expected. Sara Cartlaigne had lived her life exactly as she'd wanted and would welcome pity from no one.

After a sip or two of the coffee and juice had been taken, the tray was removed. Toni did several other small things to make her aunt comfortable, then picked up the tray and left the room.

"Aunt Ellen seems to be the one in Aunt Sara's thoughts today," she remarked as she entered the kitchen. She set the tray on the counter, then emptied the glass and cup and placed them in the dishwasher. "She never did recognize me."

"Try not to let it upset you, honey," Mrs. D said, patting Toni's shoulder. "The doctor assures me she's in no pain."

"Oh, Mrs. D . . . I'm not really upset." Toni sighed. "I can't honestly say I'd want to hold on to her if she couldn't continue her life as she has. I understand her deep sense of pride and that feeling of independence she's blessed . . . or cursed with. I'm just glad I came when I did. Perhaps I'm also being selfish. She's always been special to me . . . my talisman, you might say."

"I understand, my dear. But when that time does come, you'll weather it with the same pride and independence your aunt possesses. Now," she added, deftly switching the conversation to a less emotional topic, "I think I'm ready to visit Mr. Barr."

"From the looks of that basket, you have enough food to keep him supplied for a week."

"Nonsense," Mrs. D said as she grasped the two sturdy handles of the wicker container and headed for the door. "A man needs nourishment."

After she'd gone, Toni set about straightening the kitchen and spent some time with her aunt, helping the older woman decide what to wear for her visit with the doctor. Later, as she wandered through the house looking for something to keep her busy, her thoughts centered on her bank balance which, without the weekly deposit of a paycheck, was beginning to dwindle.

Her spur-of-the-moment desire to visit Natchez had been just that. She hadn't thought beyond getting away from a situation that had been embarrassing and painful for her. Now she was faced with paying rent on an apartment she wasn't using, and worrying about her furniture.

She could depend on Connie to look after things for her, and Toni knew her friend was expecting her to return to Richmond eventually. But with Aunt Sara rapidly losing ground, Toni wouldn't even consider leaving.

Getting a job like the one she'd had in Richmond would be impossible, leaving her with no other alternative but to seek a secretarial position.

"I'll remember to mention it to Susie," she murmured, just as the back door opened and Mrs. D walked in.

"Well?" Toni asked alertly. "Is he still growling like a grouchy bear?"

"Not at all, poor dear," the kindly woman answered. She set the hamper down on the counter, then faced Toni. "He's the most charming gentleman I've ever met."

Toni looked at the housekeeper, then out the window and back to the housekeeper. "I suppose someone could have switched bodies during the night," she said thoughtfully. "The Christian Barr I'm acquainted with is definitely not a charming gentleman."

"Ah, you young folks and your strange ideas," Mrs. D scoffed. "That young man is a treasure. And just between you and me, I think he's in considerable pain. I offered to call Brent, but he wouldn't let me. I think you should go over there and see if you can talk some sense into him."

"I'm sure he'll manage," Toni replied, unconcerned, but she remembered the glazed look of pain she'd seen in his eyes the evening before. She also had no trouble remembering being in Christian's arms and the feel of his lips against hers.

"Nevertheless, Toni, you should go over there and try," Mrs. D said worriedly. "After all, it was our goat that caused the poor man to be in this condition."

"All right, Mrs. D." Toni patted the woman's hand consolingly. "There's no need to pull out your crying towel. I'll go. By the way," she said with a grin as she started toward the door, "my aunt seems to have regained her faculties enough to demand her purple velvet dress. I hesitated at the plumed creation she called a hat, and decided to leave that little problem in your capable hands."

"Oh, my." Mrs. D sighed. "That dear lady has the most . . . er . . . the most remarkable taste I've ever seen when it comes to hats. I'd hoped she would have forgotten some of her more colorful ones."

When Toni reached the side entrance of the big house, she raised her fist and knocked loudly on the door. A gruff command to enter left her no choice but to open the door and go in. She'd have much preferred having her short conversation on the porch rather than inside.

"Did your conscience get to bothering you or did Mrs. D shame you into coming over?" Christian asked from directly behind her.

Toni gave a startled gasp at the sound of his voice. She swung around and saw the "patient" leaning against the casement of one of the floor-to-ceiling windows that flanked the door. His position had afforded him a perfect view of her as she'd approached the house.

"Neither," she glibly lied, her dark eyes running over the tall length of him. Heavens! He was absolutely huge. He was dressed in faded jeans and a plaid shirt that was unbuttoned with the tail hanging loosely about his hips. "I've been busy this morning and this is the first chance I've had to run over."

Christian didn't move from his position as his dark-blue gaze reacquainted itself with each inch of her figure before coming to rest on her face. "I thought we'd cleared up the need for lies between us last night."

Every hair on the nape of Toni's neck stood on end at the mention of the previous evening. He didn't believe in wasting time, did he? "I wasn't aware that we had anything that needed clearing up between us. Perhaps my memory isn't as good as yours. All I recall is you being left with a fuzzy head after the shot Brent gave you."

And that, mister, is all I'll admit to, she silently vowed.

"You've forgotten that I kissed you? That you responded warmly and beautifully? I told you our affair would be something you'd never forget . . . or words to that effect."

Without batting an eye, Toni calmly pushed back the sleeve of the green sweater she was wearing and looked at her watch. "It's twenty past nine. My aunt's appointment with her doctor is at ten fifteen. That leaves us with approximately fifty-five minutes to begin, and end the shortest affair on record." Toni was lying through her teeth about the time of the appointment and her taking Aunt Sara to the doctor, but she had to beat him at his own game. She glanced toward the sofa, then back to a scowling Christian. "Do you prefer sofas or beds for these little interludes in your life?"

"Am I supposed to applaud or turn you over my

knee?" he asked in a silky voice that barely hid the steel beneath.

Toni watched him take three slow, deliberate steps toward her, and knew a quiet moment of panic as she bravely stood her ground. "I really don't think either is necessary. I was simply giving you a dose of your own medicine," she said quietly. "Now you have some idea of how I feel when you start making ridiculous comments about 'our' affair."

By then Christian was standing directly in front of her. Try as she might, Toni was unable to keep her gaze from his tanned chest and the short dark hair that covered it and narrowed out of sight beneath the waistband of his pants.

It was as though human skin had taken on some new and important meaning for her as she stared. Her hands became tight fists of restraint against the almost uncontrollable urge to reach out and trail her fingertips against him.

When she suddenly felt his touch against her neck and felt the inevitable pull toward him, she looked into his eyes, only to lose herself in their enigmatic glow.

She raised one small hand in protest, only to have it become pressed against the strong chest that had so fascinated her only seconds before. The beat of Christian's heart, rapid and strong, pounded against her palm.

"This is . . . ridiculous," she barely managed in a shaky voice that bore no resemblance to her normal tone.

"I don't agree," Christian whispered as his arms swallowed her and his lips claimed hers.

Toni knew the war was lost before the battle ever began. His large, powerful hands pressed her against him, flattening her breasts against his chest. Instead of storming the softness of her mouth, as she expected, he traced the generous curve of her lips with his tongue, teasing her, making her desire grow more intense.

Each time the silken tip came near its mark, Toni prepared to welcome it. It became a titillating game of tempt and run till, on fire for more than a teasing moment, she put an end to his playful wanderings.

She somehow managed to disentangle her hands from between their bodies, then raised both to grasp Christian's head. This time, when his tongue completed its dalliance at the corner of her lips and lazily began to inch its way to the fuller, more sensuous center, her own honeyed tongue met it.

The sudden plunge she'd been eagerly awaiting came, and with it, a light-headedness that had her hands sliding down and grasping his broad shoulders for support. She invited him deeper into the exciting darkness of her mouth, completely giving herself over to the desperate need that sprang up within her. She knew that the merging of their mouths was only a prelude to a deeper urgency that was slowly enveloping her.

Suddenly it was as though the floor were being ripped from beneath their feet by a loud knocking on the door. Christian raised his head, his eyes dark with the same intense glow that marked Toni's. He ran his hands possessively over her hips and back, letting them stop beneath her arms, against the sides of her warm, tingling breasts.

"I could easily kill whoever is standing on the other side of that door," he rasped in a husky voice. He raised one hand and curved it to the side of Toni's face, then bent and touched his lips to her forehead. "Don't you dare leave," he whispered. "We definitely have some unfinished business to discuss."

He stepped back then and hastily began to tuck his shirt into his trousers and button it.

Toni turned away from the bold, knowing expression on his rugged face, her hands instinctively smoothing her dark hair.

By the time Christian opened the door, she felt she had at least one foot on the ground. She only hoped the visitor wasn't too careful in noting the rosy glow she knew was in her cheeks.

Whatever hopes she'd had of appearing calm and unflustered, however, were dashed the moment she heard Susie's voice and saw Christian step back and invite her cousin in.

Susie swept into the room, armed with a large covered dish, and immediately sized up the situation. She leveled a sharp-eyed glance at Toni, smiled smugly, then turned to Christian, who was just behind her.

"This is such a terrible thing to happen to you," she began in that flighty way that usually had people thinking her head held nothing more substantial than sawdust. "When Brent told me about your accident and that there was no one to cook for you, I thought you might enjoy this." She thrust the dish toward him.

"Thank you," Christian said with his customary charm. "Between you and Mrs. D, I'll probably have to start jogging again." He included both women in a broad smile and said, "Excuse me while I take this to the kitchen."

The very instant his back disappeared from view, Susie flew to Toni's side and clutched her arm. "I simply couldn't believe your good fortune when Brent got back and told me who your new neighbor was. Isn't he fabulous?"

"If you say so," Toni remarked dryly, then tried to change the subject. "Did you stop in and see Aunt Sara?"

"I'll do that later," Susie said dismissively. "What do you mean, 'If I say so'? Have you lost your mind? Christian Barr is the type of man any woman would kill for."

"I guess he'd be a good catch," Toni conceded. "But he moves a little too fast for me. We'd be like the tortoise and the hare."

"Then have your engine overhauled, honey, because this one is dynamite," her cousin fussed.

"Don't be so pushy, Susie. I'm not a rubber ball, ready to bounce from one man to another. I came here for some peace and quiet, and to straighten out my life."

"What you've done, Antonia Elizabeth, is let that Steven Crowell turn you against all men. You're just stubborn enough to want to end up exactly like Aunt Sara."

"Would that really be so bad?" Toni asked, unable to keep from teasing Susie.

"It would be horrible and I won't stand for it. I intend to see you happily married if it's the last thing I do," the harassed blonde hissed in a furious undertone just as Christian entered the room bearing a tray.

"I hope you ladies will join me for a cup of coffee?" he said politely. Susie rushed forward and relieved him of his burden, then placed it on the large oval table in front of the extra-long sofa.

"We'd love to," she replied, so enthusiastically that Toni was tempted to apply some of the same measures she'd used against her flighty cousin as a child . . . starting with a swift kick in the rear!

I will not be manipulated, she thought stormily as she watched Christian sprawl comfortably on the sofa with Susie seated in a chair to his right. Toni took a step forward as though accepting the invitation, then paused behind a chair.

She rested her hands on the tall back and assumed what she hoped was a proper expression of regret. "A cup of coffee sounds like heaven, but it's almost time for Aunt Sara's appointment."

"I thought Mrs. D was taking her," Susie said.

"We've had to alter our usual plans somewhat," Toni lied without a trace of remorse. She met the chilling "You'll be sorry" look in Christian's eyes with an unconscious tilt of her small stubborn chin. "Why don't you take your doctor's advice and rest. You've been far too active this morning. I'll see both of you later."

As she scooted through the tall hedges, Toni felt a sense of overwhelming relief. Her brief encounter with Christian the night before was nothing compared to what Susie had interrupted.

Getting within six feet of the damned man was proving to be as dangerous as going over Niagara Falls in a brown paper bag. She decided she would have to arrange their future meetings in such a way as to eliminate the intimate little encounters that seemed to keep occurring between them.

Brent had advised Christian to take it easy for a couple of days. *So,* Toni concluded as she neared the back door of the cottage, *that leaves a day and a half to get through. I sincerely hope Mrs. D can cope, for nothing short of Christian Barr being near death will get me alone with him again.* "As for my cousin," Toni murmured out loud, plotting in her mind a suitable revenge, "I'll probably choke her."

But at that precise moment Susie was doing her best to play Cupid. After Toni's hurried exit from the room, she favored Christian with a sweet, apologetic smile. "I do hope your feelings aren't hurt by my cousin's rather strange behavior."

"Not at all," he assured her as he accepted the cup of coffee she offered him. "She seems to be preoccupied, as though something's bothering her," he said with a perfectly straight face.

"Oh, she is," Susie rushed to explain. "She became engaged to an awful man shortly after her parents died. Right before she came to us, she found out that her fiancé was seeing another woman. The poor dear was crushed. She's such a gentle, frail person, the whole ordeal was almost too much for her to endure."

"Indeed," Christian soberly intoned, struggling to keep from laughing as he remembered "gentle and frail" Antonia all but beheading her fiancé. "I'm sure you're a great comfort to her."

"Oh, I mean to be more than that." Susie grinned mischievously. "I fully intend to see my cousin married before she has a chance to leave Natchez."

Christian sat back and listened to the woman recount her plans to get Toni married off. One part of him was amused by her antics; another part of him was not at all pleased that there would shortly be a succession of men parading through Antonia's life.

"Well?" Susie asked later that evening as soon as she got Toni alone in the kitchen on the pretext of helping her serve dessert. "What do you think of Raymond?"

"He's . . . nice."

"Which means?"

"He's bossy, opinionated, and a large pain in the behind," Toni said bluntly as she added hot raisin sauce to the pudding she was spooning into some dessert dishes. "As much as I love you, Susan Louise, I'm not sure I'm looking forward to meeting any more of the eligible bachelors of your acquaintance."

"Don't back out now," her cousin said with a very serious expression on her face. "I haven't even begun my campaign." She reached for a tray, added the four desserts, then grinned at Toni. "To be honest with you, though, Raymond is at the bottom of my list. But he was the only one I could get on such short notice."

"Thanks a lot," Toni muttered. "I feel exactly like some old frump you're trying to unload. If Raymond is the best you can do, sweetie, then I'm positive I'd rather live a single life."

"No, no, no," Susie said with determination. "I'll see you married off if I have to invite every single man in the state to dinner."

"Why on earth are you so obsessed with the idea of seeing me shackled to some man?"

"Because you're intelligent, pretty, and have a lot to offer some lucky guy. I also don't want you feeling inadequate or unlovable because of what happened with that wimp Steven."

Toni leaned one elbow on the surface of the counter and looked at her cousin fondly. "You know, Susie, there are times when you truly amaze me."

Susie stared down at the tray, then at Toni, a combination of love and understanding in her blue eyes. "Even though we're as different as day and night, we've always been closer than sisters, Toni. And although you've put up a great front, I can tell you're hurting." They continued to stare at each other for several seconds, smiles of understanding all the communication they needed.

"Well," Toni finally said, "let's see if dear old Raymond can dispose of this pudding as quickly as he did the casserole."

Not only did Raymond polish off the dessert as if he hadn't had a morsel of food in days, but he endlessly related to Toni the success he enjoyed in breeding and showing his German shepherds.

It didn't take Brent and Susie long to realize Raymond was totally smitten with Toni and wasn't about to allow anyone to deprive him of one single minute of her time. Finally they gave up their attempts at conversation. They had no recourse but to sit back, smother their grins, and hope Toni wouldn't seek revenge immediately after dinner.

When it came time to end the evening, Toni almost choked at Raymond's insistence that he follow her home.

She assured him that it wasn't necessary and that she was an excellent driver. Brent and Susie also did their best to dissuade him, but Raymond was adamant. And as she drove the few miles back to Cartlaigne, Toni steadily cursed the twin beams of light reflected in her rearview mirror, and her darling cousin's penchant for matchmaking.

On reaching her destination, Toni quickly grabbed her keys and purse and was out of her car well before her escort drew to a stop. She rushed back to bid him a firm good night.

"Now, you don't really think I'm going to let our

evening end this way, do you?" He smiled broadly as he opened the door and stepped out.

"Well, I can't see why not," Toni said shortly. She'd had enough of Raymond, his voracious appetite, and his damn dogs. "My aunt isn't feeling well and I really can't ask you in." That wasn't exactly the truth. She was free to have guests at any time. But not this evening, and definitely not Raymond.

"Then we'll take a walk," he suggested, reaching out and dropping a heavy arm across her shoulders.

"But it's foggy and damp, as well as being a little chilly."

"Exercise will do us good after that delicious dinner Susie cooked," he continued, ignoring Toni's protests.

"Really, Raymond, I—"

"Your aunt has been asking for you, Antonia," came a stern, deep voice from the shadows of the overgrown barrier that separated the two houses. "I hardly think she would approve of you lurking in the dark like some fifteen-year-old."

Toni's first reaction upon hearing Christian's voice was an overwhelming sense of relief. For once in his worthless life he was serving a useful purpose, or so it seemed, judging by her date's reaction.

"Who on earth is that?" Raymond asked in a stage whisper, jerking his arm away as if it had been burned.

Toni chewed thoughtfully at her bottom lip for a moment, then turned back to Raymond. "My aunt employs a small but efficient staff. They're very loyal to the family."

"I see." Raymond nodded, catching a glimpse of the man shrouded by the bushes. "Perhaps we'll take a raincheck on that walk." He laughed nervously. Before she could reply, he grabbed a startled Toni, pulled her against him, then planted a hard kiss on her lips.

A muttered "By damn, that rips it!" and the sharp rustling of bushes accounted for Toni's instant release.

Raymond did an about-face, jumped into his car, and reversed the entire distance down the long, curving driveway.

"I do not care to see you mauled by the likes of that slimy bastard!" Christian roared at Toni as he cleared the barrier and came face-to-face with her.

"Well, if you kept your shades down on this side of the house, you wouldn't have that problem," she threw at him. Her initial feeling of gratitude toward him had vanished and was now replaced by anger. Who did he think he was, telling her what she could and couldn't do? "I've no intention of conducting my social life to please you."

"Not even if it also pleases you?" Christian asked in a quiet voice. "I'll admit our relationship seems to have gotten off to a bumpy start, Antonia, but I do mean to become a very visible part of your future."

Toni stamped one foot impatiently. "We do not have a relationship, bumpy or otherwise. And *you* have about as much chance of becoming a part of my future as a snowball has in hell."

Without another word, she whirled around and ran toward the safety of the cottage.

Christian stood staring after her, one large hand thoughtfully pulling at his chin. Antonia Grant was proving to be something of a challenge. A slow grin tugged at the corners of his sensuous mouth as he saw his plans for her quick seduction fall by the wayside.

Knowing she would be in Natchez had clinched his decision as to where to spend his time off. He'd visualized numerous idyllic evenings beneath a southern moon, with the scent of magnolias filling the air as he swept his "prize" off her feet and into his bed.

Unfortunately he hadn't counted on such open hostility. It was a new and rather novel experience, having a woman thumb her nose at him.

Further introspection, however, gradually changed his grin to a puzzled frown. Connie had told him that Antonia was through with Steven Crowell. But was she? Was it possible that she was still in love with that two-timing bastard? Even Susie had said Antonia was still hurting. Would that hurt create a wall between her and her ability to enjoy a normal relationship with a man?

He wasn't at all pleased with this last thought. She deserved a man who would love and protect her . . . a man who would cherish and spoil her. At that moment Christian resolved that he would be that man, that he would be the one to wipe away all the hurt and disappointment Toni had suffered.

CHAPTER SEVEN

"How's the patient?" Susie asked, sighing with anticipation as Toni placed a thick slice of Mrs. D's fresh coconut cake before her.

"Driving me crazy," Toni answered with a frown. She sat down opposite her cousin, then reached for her coffee. "He's milking his injury for everything it's worth. I've already been over there three times today and it's only eleven thirty."

"Well, today is the third day and his need for a nurse is over." Susie grinned.

Toni leveled a narrow look at her cousin. "I fail to see the slightest bit of humor in this entire situation. As you know, the doctor said after Aunt Sara's last visit that her health is failing rapidly. That means there's no telling how long I'll be here, stuck with that pest next door."

"Don't let him bother you," Susie told her. "I've got your evenings planned for the next two weeks. I've never enjoyed anything as much. Although for the life of me, I can't understand why you feel toward Christian as you do. If you would set your mind to it, you could become Mrs. Barr before Christmas."

"Good Lord!" Toni exclaimed. "I honestly believe you still think children are found under cabbage leaves. That man isn't interested in marriage . . . and for that matter, neither am I. All he wants is to add another notch to his bedpost. Is that what you think I need?"

Susie chewed her cake, her face screwed up into such a thoughtful expression that Toni was tempted to giggle. "Why not? There are a lot worse things that could happen to you."

"I can't think of a single one at the moment."

"You're being stubborn."

"It's an inherited trait."

"All right, you win." Susie threw up her hands. "I'll continue to supply you with dross while you ignore the gold next door."

"Thank you." Toni smiled icily. "That's the best news I've heard in days."

They finished their cake and coffee, and while Susie went in to visit with Aunt Sara, Toni grabbed the grocery list Mrs. D had left on the table and slipped out the door.

Just as she reached her car, she was hailed by Christian, who was coming down the steps of the big house.

"Are you by any chance going into town?" he asked, shrugging into a light tan jacket as he stopped beside her.

"I'm going to the grocery store and the drugstore and I have to stop at the cleaners. Would you like me to pick up something for you?" she asked, a note of resignation in her voice. Was she to have him tied around her neck like a stone for the rest of her life? It just wasn't fair, especially considering how rested he appeared. He looked as if he'd spent a week at some expensive health spa, she thought maliciously.

Her gaze slipped over him from his crisp dark hair to the shiny tips of his shoes in an effort to find a single jarring note in his appearance. Finding nothing but a disturbingly attractive man in dark tan pants and a brown knit shirt, she gave up . . . for the moment.

"Do I pass inspection?" Christian asked, amused. He hadn't moved or made any attempt to speak during her critical scrutiny.

"Yes."

"Do you mind if I hitch a ride? I need to do some shopping, and it seems foolish for each of us to drive."

"You'll have to ride in my car," she reminded him in hopes he would change his mind.

"No problem. Surely a trip to town and back won't be so bad." He smiled pleasantly, although there was little fondness in his blue eyes as he turned and stared at the small car.

Several minutes later Toni was zooming down the highway, her passenger sitting beside her like a huge block of granite. The only movement from him came as he kept a watchful eye on the speedometer.

"Do you always drive this fast?" Christian asked the fourth time they passed another vehicle.

"Usually. Why? Am I making you nervous?"

"Hell yes," he answered bluntly. "I feel like I'm hurtling down the road in a cookie jar."

"Shame on you." Toni couldn't help but laugh. "I'll have you know I've never even gotten a parking ticket. And we're only going ten miles over the speed limit."

"Miracles do happen," he remarked dryly.

Toni ignored the tiny jab, interested only in getting

the trip over with as quickly and uneventfully as possible.

Whatever secret desire she'd had to see Christian at a disadvantage in the supermarket, fizzled out after the first five minutes. Not only did he compare prices, but he read the contents of each product he bought as though he expected to be quizzed on the subject at the checkout counter.

To add insult to injury, he calmly removed several items Toni had chosen, replacing them with what he considered better buys.

"But I don't want such a large jar of peanut butter," she protested. "I'll be ninety years old before I finish it off."

"I'll help you," he calmly replied. "Peanut butter and jelly sandwiches happen to be one of my favorites."

"Oh?" she asked innocently. "I don't recall inviting you to share my peanut butter."

"You haven't actually said the words," Christian said as he read the label on one can, then exchanged it for another and placed it in his shopping cart. "But I know the signs, Antonia," he said with a perfectly straight face. "I can tell when a woman is lusting after my body."

"Why, you egotistical ass!" she stormed at him, momentarily forgetting where they were. This fact was quickly brought home to her by an outraged woman, who glared at Toni, gave a muttered "Well, I never!" then grabbed her cart and marched down the aisle.

Toni watched in embarrassed silence and then looked helplessly at Christian, who was nearly choking with suppressed laughter. Harsh accusations sprang readily to her lips, only to disappear as her own sense of humor took over.

Finally, when he could speak again, Christian looped a casual arm about her shoulders and gave her a brief, hard hug. "I never knew grocery shopping could be so entertaining, Antonia. But I don't know why I'm surprised. Since meeting you, I've been party to a number of remarkable events."

Toni gave him a cheeky grin, her heart racing like a runaway train. "I did warn you . . ."

"Ahhh," he said with a nod, "so you did. But think of all I'd be missing if I had given up so early. Any minute now I expect you to fall into my waiting arms."

And from the way my heart is racing, you have no idea how close to the truth you are, she thought ruefully. It would probably be the easiest thing she'd ever done, to give in to the powerful attraction she felt for Christian. But once the attraction waned, what then?

"You're shameless, do you know that?" she said, attempting a stern reproach.

"Of course," he agreed as they began to move down the long aisle. "Did you think I'd gotten where I am today by being Mr. Nice Guy?"

"Your professional life is one thing. Do you make it a practice to employ the same tactics in your private life?"

"Are you referring to my relationship with women?"

She shrugged. "I suppose so."

"Then I'm sure you will be flattered to know that you're the first female who has refused to fall in with my way of thinking regarding how best to spend a few quiet, delightful hours. I'm usually far more successful."

"Bragging doesn't become you," she said as she gave him a disapproving look.

"Nor is it a habit I indulge in, honey. But like it or not, there are a lot of women who are looking for a good time just as much as a man," Christian stated without the slightest hesitation.

"Aren't you at all bothered by the fact that somewhere in your *busy* past you might have left behind a woman who cared deeply for you?" she asked curiously.

"Not at all. They knew the rules before the game started. No commitments, and we were each free to go at any time."

Perhaps his parents' marriage had been especially unsuccessful, she decided, and told him so.

"Quite the contrary, actually. My parents are still very much in love. They've been together over forty years and have raised five children."

"I see," Toni mumbled, a frown touching her brow. How was it possible for someone with such a background as his to be so cynical regarding women?

It was a thought that stayed with Toni as they finished their shopping, then took care of the other errands on Mrs. D's list and returned to Cartlaigne.

When Toni stopped the car in the drive at the cottage, Christian asked her to have dinner with him that evening.

"I'm sorry, but I have plans," she said with all honesty, and found that she really was sorry. Toni had to admit that being with Christian, stormy though it usually was, made her feel more alive than she ever had before.

"Is Cousin Susie still trying to unload you on some poor unsuspecting clod?" he asked, scowling.

"Looks that way." She smiled brightly, deciding to use a bit of his own philosophy against him. "But don't worry about some poor unsuspecting clod being trundled off to the altar before he realizes what's happening, Christian. With the exception of one slight deviation, I find that, like you, I like to play the field. It makes the game far more interesting. Don't you agree?"

"Not if you're going to play with wimps like Raymond." His eyes darkened and his lips became a straight, disapproving line.

"Oh, but tonight I'm seeing Mark. He's an architect and is supposed to be rolling in money," Toni said innocently. "There's no telling what kind of expensive trinkets I might get from him if I play my cards right."

This was too much for Christian. He thrust open the door and climbed out of the small car like an enraged bear. He then turned and snatched his groceries from the backseat, giving Toni the full benefit of his frigid gaze. "There's a name for women who perform favors for expensive trinkets, Miss Grant. You'd do well to think about that before giving so freely of yourself."

Without another word, he turned on his heel, stalked around the front of the car, and charged through the barrier.

Toni opened her door and stepped lightly to the ground, a mischievous grin on her face. So Christian didn't think of love and sex quite as casually as she had assumed. How interesting. Or was it, her practical side suggested, just that he was peeved because he thought he wouldn't be the recipient of her favors?

But whatever the reason for his anger, Toni was amused. She'd found a weak spot in the seemingly impenetrable hide of her neighbor. And knowing the effect the wretch had on her, she needed all the ammunition she could gather to keep him at bay.

The remainder of the day passed quickly as Toni helped Mrs. D about the house and then read to Sara. Her aunt's condition didn't seem to be improving, and that saddened Toni. At one point she even considered canceling her date, but the housekeeper wouldn't hear of it.

"There isn't a thing you can do for your aunt, honey. And if she were able, she would be the first to tell you so. You've stayed in this house too much as it is."

"All right," Toni said with a sigh. "I'll go. But I've left a number where I can be reached if you need me. Susie and Brent will be there also."

"Stop thinking about telephone numbers and being needed, child," Mrs. D said sternly. "You're young and pretty. Go out and enjoy life. Although, if I were you, I wouldn't go a step farther than next door."

"You and Susie." Toni rolled her eyes upward. "The two of you must be Christian's greatest fans."

"I know," the housekeeper said, slowly shaking her head, "you have your reasons, or so you think. But I say there's a great deal more to that man than the reputation you're so afraid of."

"I'll keep that in mind," Toni said as she headed to her room to get dressed. She'd learned that once Mrs.

D got started singing Christian's praises, it was almost impossible to stop her.

Mark Arnold turned out to be one of the nicest men Toni had ever met. He talked about his career, but not incessantly as Raymond had done.

"I suppose you could say that being an architect is similar to being a writer or a painter. We each have a need for self-expression, but we've all chosen different ways to achieve it," he explained.

He and Toni were perched on a window seat away from the general noise of the party.

As they talked on, Mark seemed very interested in how long Toni planned to stay in Natchez. She explained that she'd resigned her position with the television station in Virginia and wasn't certain of her future plans. Without being specific, she talked about her parents' death and her need to get away. She made no mention, though, of the fact that a broken engagement had been the real reason for her trip south.

The party ended and Mark saw her home, and Toni gauged the evening a success. The only blemish had been the odd moments when, without the slightest warning, Christian Barr's angry face had crowded her thoughts.

Once they reached Cartlaigne, they remained in the car for a few minutes, each seeming to enjoy having found someone so easy to talk to.

"I must admit this is one blind date I'm glad I accepted," Mark said with a grin. "When Susie called me, I was skeptical."

"Don't apologize." Toni laughed. "I've been caught in that same trap a number of times myself. It seems that everybody has a friend or a relative coming to town who needs a date."

"Will you have dinner with me one evening next week? I can't be more specific right now because I'm expecting to have to go out of town."

"I'd like to," Toni answered, smiling. "Give me a call later and we'll—"

Whatever else she was about to say was broken off by the blinding light that caught them full face.

"What on earth is that?" Mark asked, raising one hand protectively over his eyes.

"My aunt's caretaker," Toni said through clenched teeth, the urge to kill uppermost in her mind. "He has a cute little habit of roaming the grounds at all hours." She bid Mark a rather hurried good night, then got out of the car. "Don't worry about seeing me to the door," she said hastily. "This character is so weird, he'd probably ask you to leave."

"Are you certain it's safe for you?"

"Oh, yes," Toni assured him in a loud voice. "Mr. Barr harbors a vengeance against the entire world because he's getting old. I've been told that in his younger days he was something of a ladies' man. My aunt keeps him around because of a close friendship with his family."

"Well, if you're sure," Mark said cautiously.

Toni waited until the taillights of Mark's car were out of sight and then raced like a small tornado toward Christian. "Turn off that damned floodlight," she lashed out angrily as she approached her tormentor. Immediately the light was doused.

"Just what in hell do you think you're doing?" She glared up at him.

"Why, it's simple, Antonia," Christian said calmly.

"Since there's no man living in your aunt's house, I think it's my duty to make certain you get in safely in the evenings."

"You can take your duty, Christian Barr, and go straight to hell. I neither need nor want your protection!" she nearly screamed at him.

"Surely you wouldn't begrudge an *old* man who's burned himself out with the ladies a chance to perform one last decent act, would you?" And though Christian's tone seemed frivolous enough, Toni caught the steely edge of anger underneath.

How dare he get angry, she silently raged. He wasn't the one being subjected to a flaming idiot, stalking the grounds at night and scaring her guests half to death. To her way of thinking, she was the injured party, and the right to express anger was her personal privilege.

"Even if your intentions were honorable, which I know they aren't, I'd like to point out that I'm over twenty-one and quite capable of conducting my social life without you standing in the background, peering over my shoulder."

"That's debatable," Christian replied stiffly, and Toni knew, even though she couldn't see him clearly, that his jaw was set and his eyes stormy. "You're still recovering emotionally from an experience that's left you vulnerable. What you need now is a man mature and strong enough to make you realize what a fantastic woman you really are. You certainly don't need this continuous round of 'available' bachelors groping at you in parked cars."

"Oh? How interesting," Toni answered, her expression grim. "Am I to conclude from your pompous remarks that you consider yourself the ideal man to step in and make me feel like a woman and restore my flagging sense of self-worth?"

"Of course I am." Confidence oozed from his voice. "And you'd know it too if you'd get off this ridiculous merry-go-round your cousin's put you on, long enough to see what's going on."

"You really are serious, aren't you?" she asked uncomfortably. Toni's instincts warned her that she was standing on very shaky ground. She knew she could handle an angry Christian, even an unscrupulous one, but certainly not a calm, quiet one, saying things she knew to be true.

"I've never been more serious in my entire life, Antonia," he said quietly.

Before she could guess his next move, she felt his hand slip over hers. "Come inside and have something warm to drink."

Warning bells of every conceivable size and shape clanged inside Toni's head. But what harm could one innocent drink bring? she asked herself, then refused to let her mind dwell on the obvious answer.

"Lead on, Mr. Barr." She smiled up at him in the darkness. "You have a very thirsty woman on your hands."

Several minutes later they were sitting on the sofa, sipping brandy before a softly flickering fire.

The brandy, the fire, and Christian's hard thigh pressed against hers combined to loosen Toni's tongue. She was answering each question he asked her without hesitation.

"So you really aren't certain when or if you'll be returning to Richmond, are you?" Christian asked.

"Not really. I've been thinking about looking for a

secretarial position here in Natchez, but with my aunt not feeling well, I haven't done anything about it."

"Susie mentioned that you're very close to Miss Cartlaigne. I'd like to meet her."

Toni smiled. "My mother, and now my cousin, always accused me of being exactly like Aunt Sara. And," she added with a shrug, "I suppose I am."

"Then I really must meet this charming individual." Christian grinned. "Does she have the same remarkable ability to make things happen as you do?"

"Oh, Aunt Sara far surpasses me," Toni told him with a merry twinkle in her dark eyes. She related the story of the tiny woman taking the horsewhip to her intended, and also the one about her aunt's fondness for her trusty shotgun.

"It's a pity she's not well," Christian said thoughtfully. "She could get in quite a bit of target practice with the different men parading in front of her door of late."

"You're rude and overbearing," Toni accused him without any real malice in her voice. "If I didn't know better, I'd swear you and my aunt were in cahoots regarding my escorts."

"A man will do any number of seemingly strange things when he's interested in a woman," Christian said, an amused look on his face. "It's a rare form of temporary insanity."

"Insanity my foot!" Toni exclaimed with a frown. "I'd call it premeditated mischief. By now, I'm sure word has gotten around that taking me home from a date is considered dangerous."

"Ahhh . . . what a shame," Christian said as innocently as a small boy, his laughing gaze meeting and holding hers. "Does it upset you that I might have created a temporary lull in your social life?"

"No, you fink, I'm not upset. Annoyed? Yes. I don't like being manipulated. And from what I've seen of you, Mr. Barr, you're accustomed to doing just that if people don't react as you want them to."

Christian reached for her hand and raised it to his lips. "If I very humbly apologize, will it help?"

Toni felt a strange new excitement rushing through her veins. The fire crackling in the grate was nothing compared to the one raging inside her, brought on by his touch, his nearness.

"How can I be certain you mean it?" she whispered in an unsteady voice against the sudden tension surrounding them.

"Perhaps this will help," he murmured huskily, then pulled her across his muscled thighs and covered her mouth with his.

The moment his tongue plunged into the sensitive softness eager to receive it, Toni found that she'd been unconsciously waiting for this since the last time he'd kissed her. Rapid spasms of pleasure raced through her body like jagged fingers of lightning on a stormy day.

She felt his hands caressing her back, her hips, then changing course to sweep over her flat stomach and upward to the tingling softness of her breasts.

It was as though she'd become two different people. One, sane and disapproving, hovering above as she watched her other self responding without hesitation to Christian's sensual touch.

Even when his hands brushed aside the tiny buttons of her dress and the fragile lace of her bra, to cup first one breast and then the other, Toni didn't pull back.

She remembered, fleetingly, that first encounter in Steven's office with Christian, when she'd compared the two men. She'd resented him then. Now that resentment had turned into a burning desire that held her securely in its grip. She clung to him, savoring the rough hunger of his large body as he moved against her.

When his lips burned a scorching trail down her neck to ultimately close over one excited nipple, a tiny gasp of pleasure escaped her mouth. Each time he touched her with his hands, with his lips, brought even more excitement than the last. Her body became as soft as a tender green leaf, bending and molding itself to the incredibly persuasive commands that issued from Christian's fingers.

When Christian raised his head and studied her glowing eyes and her softly parted lips, a gentle, tender smile stole over his strong features.

"I want to make love to you," he whispered. "I want to keep you with me for days and weeks."

Toni raised a tentative hand that finally came to rest against his cheek. Her thumb teased the curve of his lips. "Does that go along with your apology?" she asked huskily.

"Are you complaining?"

"Oh, no." She smiled. "As apologies go, I'm certain yours is the most . . . stirring one I've ever received. You have a remarkable flair for expressing yourself."

"But," he said knowingly, "you aren't ready yet, are you?"

Toni stared at this man and found, to her surprise, that discussing whether or not to go to bed with him wasn't at all embarrassing. That startling bit of information was something she'd have to think about later

. . . as well as her surprise defection to her enemy's camp.

"I accepted your apology. Will you let me work this out in my own way?"

"Only if you will promise to have dinner with me tomorrow evening."

"Oh, but—"

Christian's brows flew together across the bridge of his nose in a dark warning frown. "Don't you dare tell me you're going out with another of Susie's clones. I can be very nasty when riled."

"So can I . . . when I'm being threatened," she swiftly countered.

"Touché, Miss Grant." Christian chuckled, a quick gleam of admiration springing to his eyes. "Let me put it another way. It would please me enormously if you would stop seeing other men. How's that?"

"Much better." Toni laughed softly. "And I'd love to have dinner with you. As for not seeing other men . . ." She shrugged. "I can't promise. Let's just take it day by day. Besides, Susie might not like you interfering with her plans."

But Susie wasn't at all upset when Toni phoned to tell her of the change of plans. This left Toni with the realization that she'd done exactly as her cousin had been urging her to do.

For one tiny second after replacing the receiver, Toni was tempted to march over and tell Christian that she wouldn't be available for dinner. Further thoughts regarding the matter, however, reminded her that she'd be a fool to willingly deprive herself of his company simply because of Susie's crazy maneuvering.

The remainder of the day moved along at a snail's pace, or so it seemed to Toni. As she wandered through the house looking for something to keep her busy, she found herself, more often than not, keeping a watchful eye on the big house.

Two times Christian left in his car. On the first trip he was away for more than two hours; the second time, only forty-five minutes.

Stop it! she silently lectured herself as she watched the car stop after the last outing. *You're beginning to act like a lovesick schoolgirl!*

I wonder what my feelings really are? she asked herself, but was too cowardly to wait for the answer. Instead, she turned away from the window and went in search of Mrs. D and some chore to keep her thoughts occupied.

Early in the afternoon Sara, in one of her more lucid moments, announced that she would be eating dinner in the dining room that evening. Both Toni and Mrs. D were pleased with the news, and the housekeeper suggested that Toni might like to help her aunt dress.

After the old woman had donned her blue velvet dress, and her snowy white hair had been combed into its coronet atop her small head, Toni asked Sara if she'd like to meet their new neighbor.

"Oh? Do we have new neighbors?" Sara asked, her face showing puzzlement.

"A Mr. Christian Barr moved in about a week ago, Aunt Sara. He's asked about you several times. After dinner, if you feel up to it, I thought I'd ask him over to meet you."

"That'll be nice, dear."

Toni didn't pursue it further. She could tell by the

faraway look in her aunt's eyes and the lack of interest that Sara was already drifting back in time.

At six thirty sharp Toni heard Mrs. D open the door and let Christian in. She gave one last look at her reflection in the mirror and was pleased. Her red dress had a criss-crossed ruffled bodice. Its long sleeves gathered at the cuff, and the full skirt whispered about her knees when she moved. She picked up a delicately crocheted stole and a small clutch purse that matched the strappy black heels she was wearing, then left the room.

As she neared the sitting room Toni could hear her aunt's voice and Christian's deeper one as they talked. She paused in the doorway and smothered a grin of amusement. Their guest was seated directly in front of Sara, on an antique straight chair with legs that looked incapable of holding a child, much less a man of Christian's size.

Adding to his misery was the cup of hot coffee, served in a cup and saucer from Sara's favorite Haviland china. He had a death grip on the saucer with one hand, and the thumb and forefinger of his other hand looked to be permanently glued to the delicate handle of the cup. His uneasy posture reminded Toni of a man prepared to spring to his feet the moment the chair beneath him collapsed.

When Toni walked into the room, Sara turned her regal head and smiled and Christian rose to his feet like a jack-in-the-box. "I've been getting to know your young man, Antonia. He's very nice," Sara said in a clear voice.

Toni placed her stole and purse on the sofa, then sat on the arm of her aunt's chair. "Do you really think so, Aunt Sara?" she asked thoughtfully, her lips twitching as she watched her "young man" ease his large self back down onto the object of torture. "He has a shocking reputation with the ladies, I've been told."

"That will make him a better husband, my dear," Sara Cartlaigne said, unperturbed. "It's the paragons of virtue that you have to be careful of. Besides," she added, patting her niece on the hand, "you're a Cartlaigne through and through. A husband with a roving eye won't be a problem for one so spirited."

"Believe me, Miss Cartlaigne," Christian said to his tiny hostess, "I would never deliberately do anything to hurt Antonia. I also think I'd make an excellent husband for her," he said calmly, ignoring the angry flash in Toni's eyes. "Your niece is very impulsive by nature. She needs a watchful eye on her at all times," he added as smugly and piously as a black-frocked preacher.

Aunt Sara nodded approvingly, then instructed him to have Antonia home at a decent hour. "Young folks nowadays stay out till all hours. It's no wonder the world is going to hell in a hand basket." At that moment Mrs. D bustled in to see her charge safely to her room.

"You'll have to excuse me, Mr. Barr," Sara said to Christian. "I haven't been feeling well lately, and I find myself going to bed earlier and earlier. I've enjoyed your visit very much."

Again Christian rose to his feet. He set the cup on a small table, then stepped forward and helped Sara to her feet. "It's been my pleasure, Miss Cartlaigne," he said warmly. "Perhaps you'll be kind enough to let me come again. And please, call me Christian."

The tiny lined face broke into a bright smile, and

Toni could have sworn her aunt was flirting. "You're welcome here anytime, Christian." She turned and kissed Toni, then allowed Mrs. D to help her from the room.

Christian slowly shook his dark head and grinned at Toni. "Aunt Sara believes in speaking her mind, doesn't she?"

"And how," Toni agreed. "You were very patient with her, thank you. And please, since I'm not in the market for a husband, don't let her bluntness bother you."

He reached out and placed a long forefinger against her lips. "Shame on you, Antonia," he scolded her in mock reproof. "I wasn't at all put off by her bluntness. How could I be when she and I share such a common characteristic?"

"Oh? What's that?"

"Determination," he said quietly. "For example, I'm determined to have you, Antonia, and I don't intend to let anything or anyone get in my way."

Toni met the open directness of his gaze, a vague warning sounding in her mind. Christian had never kept it a secret that he found her an attractive woman, but in the past Toni had just thought it was part of his line. This time, however, there was no mistaking the challenge in his voice.

"Are you trying to bully me again?" she asked with a smile, unable to explain the sudden huskiness creeping into her voice.

"Perhaps." He let his hand slip behind her head and clasped the nape of her neck. "You're different from the women I've known in the past. You're a pint-size mischief maker who's managed to create complete havoc in my life. You're stubborn as a mule, and there are times I'm positive that if you were a man, you'd give me the thrashing of my life."

"You make me sound mean-tempered and somewhat odd," Toni murmured, trying to ignore the excitement his touch was creating.

"You are." Christian smiled. "But don't you dare change. You're unique."

Before she could think of a reply to this rather unusual compliment, she heard the phone ringing. A softly spoken "Excuse me" slipped past her lips as she hurried toward the kitchen.

When she answered the phone her voice was a little breathless and shaky from Christian's touch and her own confused response to him.

"Toni? This is Steven," came the familiar voice of her former fiancé. "How are you?"

"I'm fine, Steven," she answered, surprised, then found herself tongue-tied. *What on earth do I say to him?* she thought frantically.

"I suppose you're wondering why I'm calling, aren't you?" he asked in that persuasive voice she'd heard so often.

"To be quite honest, Steven, I am," Toni confessed as she reached out and pulled forward Mrs. D's stool and sat down. "Has something happened to Connie or your parents?"

"Everyone's fine, except me. I miss you, sweetheart, and I want to see you."

"See me?" she said incredulously. "What on earth for?" Even before the question was out of her mouth, she felt, rather than saw, Christian behind her. At Steven's next question, her voice took on a raspy edge. "Steven, I'm not sure I'll be returning to Richmond."

"Then may I come to Natchez?" he further shocked

her by asking. "I've been a damn fool, Toni, and I want you back."

"Really, Steven—"

"Don't say no," he interrupted. "I know now how much I hurt you. Nothing has gone right for me since you left. No matter what you say, I'm coming to see you."

"I'm afraid it will be a wasted—"

"Let me be the judge of that, sweetheart. See you soon," he said before she could finish, then hung up.

Toni sat for several seconds with the receiver pressed against her ear before hanging it up. She turned and faced Christian, her own thoughts keeping her from picking up on his annoyance.

"Something wrong?" he asked in a cold voice that startled Toni.

"Not wrong exactly." She shrugged. "As I'm sure you heard, that was Steven. He insists on coming down here."

"If you didn't want to see him, why didn't you just say so?" Christian asked with his usual bluntness.

Toni stood, still wary of the sudden iciness of his mood. "I tried, but he wouldn't listen. He can be very stubborn at times."

Christian crossed his strong arms over his chest and carefully regarded her for several moments, then asked, "Are you certain you really tried to discourage him? Maybe you're having second thoughts about breaking your engagement and leaving Richmond so abruptly."

"Are you suggesting that I'm still in love with Steven?" Toni asked, resenting his cross-examining.

"It's been known to happen."

"Well, not this time, I assure you," she said firmly.

"What Steven and I had is finished. I'd be a lot happier if he would accept that and stay in Richmond."

"If that's really the case, then he should be well on his way back to Richmond within an hour of getting here, shouldn't he?" Christian asked smoothly.

"I suppose so, but then I'm not his travel agent," she remarked darkly. "He might be interested in seeing some of the old homes while he's here."

Damn it! She didn't care at all for the way Christian was acting. Any love she'd had for Steven was dead. She knew that. But, Toni reasoned, if the man insisted on rehashing a dead issue, then so be it. It was certainly no concern of Christian's if her ex-fiancé stayed for one hour or one week.

But Christian was concerned. And as he led Toni to the car, he realized that the prospect of Steven Crowell turning up next door disturbed him greatly.

He tried not to think about it, but even the quiet elegance of dinner at the historic Eola Hotel and the soft glow of candlelight failed to wipe from his mind the thought of Toni in Steven's arms.

All through dinner there was a part of him that held back, that remained aloof from the seemingly easy conversation he was having with Toni. And it wasn't until they were leaving that it hit him. *I'm afraid of losing her,* Christian thought dazedly, then just as quickly tried to deny the idea.

But no amount of mental gyrations on his part could dislodge the mind-numbing blow: After all these years of casual relationships he had finally fallen for a woman—the one woman capable of telling him to take a hike over the edge of a mountain! What had started out as his usual dedicated but uninvolved pursuit of an attractive woman had backfired completely. Now he found himself unsure of himself and afraid of another man's influence over Antonia.

If Toni was aware of an added glow in Christian's gaze as it swept over her, or the extra warmth of his touch as he held her hand, she ignored it. It was far easier to chalk it up to the wine they'd had at dinner than to think that Christian might actually love her.

She'd misread one man's intentions before and had found out the hard way that things rarely appeared as they really were. *Besides,* she told herself, *I already know that Christian is only interested in an affair. Reading anything more into his actions would make me a fool twice over.*

When they reached Cartlaigne and Christian helped her from the car, Toni automatically turned toward the cottage. But Christian was quicker and stronger. He slipped an arm around her waist and turned her toward the big house.

"This evening isn't over yet, Miss Grant," he murmured against her ear as he ushered her toward the porch.

"My, my, aren't we masterful tonight." Toni chuckled as she allowed him to hustle her up the steps, across the porch, and into the warm, cozy sitting room.

Once inside, Christian closed the door, then leaned back against it, pulling Toni close to him. "You . . ." he whispered as his lips teased hers, "are to go over to that sofa, sit down, and wait for me while I get us a brandy."

Toni reached up and grasped the lapels of his jacket for leverage, then nipped at the fullness of his bottom lip. The wine at dinner and the warmth of his touch had removed all inhibitions as neatly as a giant eraser making a clean sweep across a blackboard.

"Are you asking me or telling me?" she whispered, pulling back at the precise moment he was going to kiss her. There was a brilliant, glowing fire in her teasing dark eyes as she looked up at him.

Christian sucked in a huge breath of air, his large hands running over her slimness as though fearful of losing her. "If I say I'm telling, I'm afraid you'll clobber me." He grinned. "So I'll be extremely polite and ask you to kindly wait for me on the sofa."

Toni's head tilted to one side as she continued to smile mischievously. "How nicely put, Mr. Barr. I will be happy to do as you ask. Only please make my brandy a small one. You were more than generous with the wine at dinner." She turned out of his arms, walked over to the sofa, and sat down, her eyes never leaving him while he removed his jacket and tie, poured the drinks, and then walked toward her.

She took the snifter and leaned back against the plush softness of the cushions.

"When is your friend supposed to arrive?" he asked as he came down close beside her. She could feel the heat of his body radiating through the thin material of her dress like a blast of hot steel along one entire side of her.

"If you're referring to Steven," she replied from her relaxed position, "then your guess is as good as mine. He didn't give me a definite time of arrival."

"Then that doesn't leave me much time, does it?"

"For what?"

"To make certain dear ol' Steven goes back to Richmond empty-handed," Christian said with a deliberateness that brought a puzzled frown to her face.

"Would you mind explaining?"

"It's simple, Antonia," he continued. He leaned forward and set his glass on the coffee table, then turned and reached for her. Suddenly Toni found herself sitting in his lap, with his arms securely locked around her.

"I've spent considerable time and effort getting to know you. I'll be damned if I'll sit calmly by and let another man whisk you from beneath my nose."

Toni felt his hand cup the nape of her neck and saw his head closing the short distance between them. When his lips took command of hers, there wasn't the slightest hesitation in her response. Thoughts of Steven's impending visit, of her own reluctance to fully trust Christian, of everything else, vanished as a hard mouth took possession of her softer yielding one.

Christian had barreled his way into her life, and though she'd tried to convince herself that he was everything she detested in a man, it simply hadn't turned out that way. The touch of his hands, the feel of his lips against hers, had become an unwitting addiction for her.

As he gently began to stroke her body, Toni knew a moment of the most intense need she had ever experienced. She pressed closer to Christian's massive chest, urgently seeking a release that only he could give her.

A gasp of pleasure burst from her lips as Christian slowly eased her dress from her shoulders. His rough palm caressed first one sensitive breast and then the other, sending little spasms of pleasure coursing through her body. Her desire was intensified as his lips closed about one taut, aroused peak, his tongue circling and teasing the nipple till Toni was certain she could no longer stand the exquisite torture.

Overcome by a rush of uncontrollable desire, Toni began to pull at the buttons of his shirt till, open at last, she ran her hands over his tanned shoulders and back. She wanted desperately to touch, to feel, to commit to memory every inch of his body. She reveled in the smell of his skin and delighted in his taste.

Suddenly there was a smothered groan from Christian. The sound barely penetrated Toni's heady world of desire and passion; neither did the feeling of being lifted by strong arms. Time held no meaning for her. All her senses were taken over with one thought—she wanted Christian Barr.

When the softness of a bed touched her bare back, Toni opened her eyes. In the dimness she recognized the large bedroom, but it wasn't the room or its beautiful antique furnishings that interested her. She could only see the man leaning over her.

"Stay with me, Antonia," he whispered.

Toni smiled, oblivious to the fact that her breasts were bare to his gaze, uncaring that a month ago he'd been nothing but a name to her. She only knew that Christian had awakened feelings and needs in her that could no longer be calmed by a few kisses or brief moments of stolen caresses.

"I'll stay . . . for a while," she whispered.

Christian's hands slowly stole to her waist, his fingers disappearing beneath the dress as he removed it. "For a while," he mused huskily as he finished undressing her. "That phrase, my dear Antonia, carries with it varied connotations."

"Tell me," Toni said softly, watching him straighten and begin to remove his own clothes. She felt no embarrassment as each piece of clothing fell to the floor, revealing the naked strength and magnificence of this man. She wanted him so urgently that her breath was coming in short painful gulps.

Rid of his last bit of clothing, Christian eased his large frame down beside her, resting his upper body on one elbow while his other hand smoothed its way back and forth across the silken skin of her stomach.

"I've been in a number of places in my travels where time isn't as important as it is in this country. So," he said with a smile, dipping his dark head to taste the fiery tip of one small nipple, "I prefer to think that 'for a while' means days, weeks, or even months."

Toni didn't bother arguing the point, but gave herself over to the almost agonizing pleasure of Christian's touch. His hands and lips seemed capable of bringing her to peaks of erotic pleasure she had never known existed.

It was as though each place he touched her, each lingering caress of his lips, was anticipated by Toni. Each gesture, each whispered endearment, whisked them closer to the final moment when he would take total possession of her body. For it seemed to Toni that he was already in possession of her soul. He eased his weight into place over her, and Toni quivered in anticipation as she arched her body against him, her slim legs becoming entangled with his tanned, hair-roughened ones.

The instant before he entered her Toni thought she would burst from desire, and when he had at last claimed her, she responded with an urgency she had never felt before. Their lovemaking was frantic, passionate, uninhibited. She felt as if she had been flung into a universe spinning out of control.

CHAPTER EIGHT

Toni juggled the packages she was carrying for what seemed like the umpteenth time. There was a frown on her face that reflected more accurately than words her impatience with her cousin, who didn't seem capable of leaving a store before she had examined each and every item it contained.

She'd been talked into coming to New Orleans to go shopping only after Brent had said Susie couldn't make the trip alone. "She has a bothersome habit of forgetting the time when she's spending money, and I don't want her driving back alone after dark."

"Do you honestly want that thing?" she finally asked Susie, who was holding and staring at an ugly mask, cast in some unknown metal. It was black and orange and hideous—or so Toni thought.

"Heavens no." Susie chuckled, then became interested in an unusual pair of candle holders.

"Are you going to buy those?" Toni nodded to the candle holders, at the same time putting up a Herculean effort not to explode.

"No." Her cousin shrugged.

"Then what in hell are you doing?" Toni stormed. "My head is aching, my arms feel like they're about to drop off, and my feet are killing me. I've watched you pick up and examine everything from baby clothes to a damn screwdriver." She glared at her cousin, her dark eyes sending out sparks of anger. "I sincerely hope someone will commit me to an institution for the mentally incompetent if I ever, ever agree to come shopping with you again!"

"Well, my goodness, Antonia Elizabeth," Susie replied in an injured tone. "There's no need to act like such a bully. I was very patient, and helpful while you were doing your shopping."

"Which I completed in less than an hour and a half. That was also before noon, Susan Louise." She maneuvered her packages in order to catch a glimpse of her watch. "It's now twenty minutes after five. Does that tell you anything?"

"You're kidding!" Susie exclaimed, checking her own watch to be sure. "Oh, my. Brent will be furious with me. We're supposed to be at the Nesbitts' by seven o'clock."

"Your husband has my heartfelt sympathy," Toni said, scowling unrepentantly.

"Oh, don't be such a grouch," Susie snapped. "I've a sneaking suspicion it's not just tired feet that's making you such a sorehead."

"My, my," Toni said grumpily as they began to weave their way through the crowded store. "Do tell me what you see in your crystal ball."

It was the first of November, and already people were starting to do their Christmas shopping.

"It's simple, cousin dear. You've been seeing more

of your handsome neighbor these last few days. Personally I think you've fallen for the man."

Toni stopped dead in her tracks and leveled a quelling stare at her relative. "How would you like to walk back to Natchez?"

"I don't think I'd care for it at all," Susie said with a grin. "Even if I do need the exercise."

"Then I suggest you keep all comments regarding Christian Barr to yourself," Toni advised. "I'm not in the mood for a cozy exchange of confidences between girls."

"Shades of Aunt Sara," Susie murmured disgustedly as they again headed for the exit. "You are determined to carry on the family tradition, aren't you?"

Toni gave an indifferent shrug of one shoulder. "I could do worse."

By the time they reached the car, Toni's feet felt like two pieces of lead. She waited while Susie unlocked the trunk of the smart Mercedes coupe, then stepped forward and unceremoniously dumped her packages inside.

"You are terrible," Susie said. She frowned and immediately leaned forward to straighten the bundles. "That lovely blouse you bought will be full of wrinkles by the time we get home."

"So will I," Toni remarked acidly.

"Honestly," the blonde woman said, and laughed. "I've never seen you in such a dark mood. Wouldn't you like to share just a teeny bit of what's bothering you?"

"You're unbelievably nosy." Toni frowned as she waited for Susie to unlock the door and then got into the car.

Susie walked around and got in on the driver's side.

"Of course I am," she said with complete candor. "How else will I know what's going on if I don't ask?"

"That's one way of looking at it, I suppose," said Toni, a rueful smile on her lips. "Unfortunately, I'm not in the mood to humor you."

Susie gave up after that, and for the next few minutes or so a companionable silence filled the car. Toni's thoughts automatically turned to Christian. It had been three days since that evening they'd made love, three days during which she'd spent countless hours attempting to sort out her feelings for him. It angered her to admit that she was no closer to figuring out the attraction he held for her than she'd been at their first meeting.

Rather than feeling at ease in his presence, she often found herself nervous and tense. Their relationship wasn't at all like the one she'd known with Steven.

Toni remembered how, after she and Steven had gotten to know each other, they'd settled into a nice, pleasant routine. There'd never been that thrill, that certain breathlessness with him, that she now felt with Christian. But then, Steven had become a part of her life during her lengthy convalescence, leaving Toni to regard him in some ways as being part of that period. That wasn't the case with Christian. Each time she saw him she felt excited and confused.

What had Toni baffled, she decided as she stared out the window of the car, was her inability to decide whether it was purely a sexual attraction she felt for Christian or something deeper, more intense.

Her dilemma wasn't helped at all by Mrs. D and Susie, who constantly harped on the subject. Added to this was also the little problem of what to do with Steven when he came to Natchez. Toni now wished that she'd been more inquisitive as to his time of arrival.

"Are you sure you won't change your mind about the Nesbitts' party this evening?" Susie asked, breaking into Toni's tangled thoughts. "There are still a number of my friends I'd like to introduce you to."

"I'm sure the party will be fantastic, but I'll meet your friends another time. I'd really like an evening in for a change."

"I suppose Christian and I have been keeping you on the go, haven't we?"

"Of course not," Toni replied airily. "Not being home in the evening for nearly two weeks is just what every woman needs." She chuckled as her sense of humor took over. Not only was Susie eager to push her into Christian's arms, but she also wasn't above introducing Toni to every unmarried man within a hundred miles in order to make Christian jealous.

There'd been moments in the last week when Toni had been amused, surprised, and angered by the ridiculous antics of her neighbor and her cousin.

Christian's latest attempt at sabotaging her plans for a pleasant few hours with one of Susie's more interesting candidates had occurred the evening before. He'd *just happened* to be out front when her date arrived.

As they drove on in silence Toni remembered that evening. She had heard the car arrive, picked up her wrap and purse, then went to tell Mrs. D she was leaving. She walked on through to the front hall, expecting any second to hear the doorbell ring.

When almost five minutes had passed and there was still no sign of her escort, she walked to the door, opened it, and stepped out onto the front porch.

"Looking for someone, Antonia?"

She turned and saw Christian, comfortably sprawled in the old-fashioned porch swing. "I thought I heard my date arrive. Perhaps I was mistaken."

"No, you weren't mistaken," Christian had said calmly. "The lawyer did arrive, but I told him you weren't feeling well."

"You did what?" she had asked quietly. She closed the door and walked over to stand directly in front of him, bringing his slow, swinging motion to a halt. Her dark eyes flashed with anger, clear warning to anyone who knew her that all definitely wasn't well.

Christian, after narrowly observing her solid stance and the taut set of her lips, had thought it more prudent to face her sitting rather than reclining. "He didn't strike me as reliable, Antonia," he had told her with a straight face, "so naturally I couldn't allow you to go out with him."

At first Toni had found herself speechless, unable to do anything but stare at him as though she hadn't heard correctly. But as the seconds ticked by and she felt her anger rising, she knew he had done exactly what he had claimed to have done. He had actually dismissed her date!

"I think it only fair to warn you, Christian," she had said in a low, tight voice, "that I'm going to kill you."

"Now? Here?"

"Oh, no," Toni had murmured in a hard, menacing voice as she moved closer, the soft material of her dress caressing his jeans-clad knee. Suddenly she reached out and pushed hard against his chest. The unexpected move and the unsteadiness of the swing had rocked a surprised Christian backward.

She quickly glanced at Susie as she smiled, remembering the shock that had registered on Christian's face. Turning her head to look out the window, she thought back to what she had done.

She had stood over him, a tiny, dark-haired bundle of rage, one hand clutching her wrap and purse, the other clenched into a tight fist which she waved beneath his nose. "Oh, no," she had repeated in an unsteady voice, her chest rising and falling with fury. "I'll get you when I'm good and ready, and when I do you'll be sorry you were ever born, let alone set foot in Natchez."

"Really, Antonia," the object of her full attention had said in a subdued voice. "I never dreamed you were so anxious to be alone with that weak-chinned weasel. He can't have gotten very far. Do you want me to get in the car and go after him?"

"No, you interfering bastard, I don't want you to do anything for me. Anything. Understand?" she had yelled at him.

"Ah, Antonia." He had smiled, then grabbed her wrist. With a quick jerk of his powerful arm, Toni felt herself tumbling forward, landing in a silken heap in his lap. "How can you say such awful things about me when you know you don't mean them?"

Knowing perfectly well that she was angry enough to hit him if given the chance, he had been careful to keep her hands in a tight grip. Toni raised her head, her hair tumbling about her face, and glared at him. "I hate you," she said through clenched teeth. "You're despicable."

Christian slowly shook his head as he stared at her. "I don't think so, honey. Angry . . . yes. But hate? No."

"And just what makes you an authority on how I

feel?" The harsh words fell effortlessly from her lips. Damn him! She was angry, and he wasn't about to get off with a few clever words and a display of caveman tactics. She wanted to inflict pain and suffering, and if she could only get her hands free, she could accomplish both goals in record time.

"It's simple, Antonia. Each time I hold you in my arms your heart beats like crazy. When I kiss you, you respond as warmly and naturally as a flower exposing its petals to the sun."

"Is that all?" she had asked stonily.

"Not on your life, sweetheart." Christian had chuckled as he touched his lips to the mutinous line of her mouth. "My ultimate weapon against your mulishness is the way you responded so beautifully to my lovemaking the other night."

A ragged sigh escaped Toni as she dragged her thoughts back to the present and tried not to remember the evening he had made love to her. She turned and stared at Susie, who was chattering away like crazy, seemingly unconcerned that her passenger wasn't hearing a word she was saying.

"Do you know if he's started?" Susie asked.

A puzzled frown settled over Toni's face as she tried to sort out the question. "I'm sorry, Susie, I'm afraid I was daydreaming. What are you talking about?"

"Christian, you nut. When I first met him, he mentioned something about doing some writing while he's here in Natchez. I was just wondering if he'd gotten started," Susie explained.

"If he has, then he's keeping it a secret." Toni frowned. "The latest form of excitement in his life is to play warden."

"So I've heard." Susie chuckled. "Personally I think

it's hilarious. I adore my husband, as you well know. But every once in a while I would appreciate something wild and crazy."

"What a pity you didn't wait a few years before marrying. If you had, then it could easily be you being driven to insanity by a madman roaming the grounds and ordering your friends away."

"Do you really mind all that much, Toni? Or are you frightened that if you do give in, you'll wind up in the same situation you did with Steven?"

"You know something, Susie? Sometimes I almost believe you understand me better than I do myself."

"Now, don't get angry with me again. I'm only trying to help."

"I'm not angry," Toni said quietly. "It's simply that you have this uncanny knack for bringing things into perspective for me. Perhaps I am afraid of turning from Steven to Christian without giving myself time to know my true feelings." She chewed at her bottom lip. "At least it's as good an excuse or reason as I've been able to come up with."

"Then would you like me to tone down my Cupid routine?" Susie said quietly. "Anyway, from Christian's reactions, it's beginning to look as though I might need to start making sure my men friends have adequate insurance coverage before I introduce them to you."

"Not yet," Toni remarked with a hint of revenge. "I don't like having my life run by someone else, especially Christian. I'll decide when and if I want to stop seeing other men." She gave her cousin a cheeky grin. "Besides, in this day and time, how can a poor girl be certain of who or what she wants if she's only allowed one choice?"

By the time they reached Cartlaigne it was dark. Susie ran in only long enough to check on her aunt, then hurried home.

Toni took her packages to her bedroom and put away the new underwear she'd bought as well as a blouse and a dress. She stared at the dress, wondering what Christian would think of it. For whether or not she cared to admit it, he'd been in her thoughts the entire time she'd been trying it on.

And that, my girl, she told herself, *is a sure sign of total idiocy or love. When a woman starts buying clothes with a certain man in mind, then I'm afraid she's got a problem.*

"So what else is new?" Toni muttered, and slammed the doors of the armoire. She felt confused and completely uncertain of which way to turn. She'd taken refuge in Steven's arms after her parents' death and her own lengthy illness. Now she seemed to be teetering on the very edge of committing the same mistake with Christian.

But affairs of the heart can't be regulated by tragedy or time or convenience, her conscience warned her. With a thoughtful expression on her face, Toni walked over to the dresser. She picked up the brush and ran it through her hair, then turned and left the room.

As she neared the kitchen, she caught the sound of Mrs. D's voice. Was Aunt Sara feeling strong enough to join them for dinner after all? For the last two days her aunt had taken a tray in her room and had been asleep by six o'clock.

But when she paused in the doorway of the kitchen, it wasn't Sara Cartlaigne the housekeeper was chatting with, but Christian. He was sitting at the long work table, a mug of steaming coffee within easy reach.

Not now, was Toni's first thought. *I need time and space.* But before she could slip quietly back into the hall and seek the security of her room, Christian turned his head, his blue gaze pinning her with compelling force.

Without taking his eyes off her he rose to his feet, resting his large, capable hands on the back of the chair. "You gals were rather late getting back from New Orleans, weren't you?" he asked in a calm voice.

Toni braced herself for what she hoped would be a short visit and walked into the room.

"If you'd ever gone shopping with my cousin, you wouldn't ask such a question." She crossed to where the housekeeper was busily preparing dinner. "Can I help, Mrs. D?"

"Everything is under control, Toni." The older woman smiled over her shoulder. "Christian's agreed to eat with us, so why don't you entertain him while I finish up? Oh, I meant to ask when you first came in. Do you want to eat in the dining room or here in the kitchen?"

"The kitchen will be fine," Toni said without thinking, not having yet recovered from the announcement that the tall, watchful man behind her was to be their guest for dinner.

She turned and faced Christian. "I think we've just been asked to leave. Why don't we settle for the sitting room before Mrs. D becomes temperamental and throws us out?"

Very good, Toni, she applauded her own performance. *Keep it cool and simple, and for goodness' sake, try to avoid becoming involved in a heavy clench with Mr. Barr. Being in his arms won't help you to work out your problems.*

When they entered the sitting room, and before Toni could put a safe distance between them, she felt Christian's arms encircle her and haul her against him. At first she tried to break his hold, but his arms tightened and his lips found their way to the wildly beating pulse at the side of her neck.

"Why are you acting like a polite stranger, Antonia?" he murmured as his lips nuzzled one ear. "I thought I made it clear to you last night that I wouldn't tolerate such actions from you."

"Please, Christian." She tried to twist her head away, knowing full well what would happen if she didn't. "I need time to think."

"You're stubborn as hell and your timing is lousy," Christian retaliated close to her ear. But for once he did as she asked and released her.

The instant his arms fell away, Toni felt as though her clothes had been stripped from her body, leaving her naked and chilled. She crossed her arms over her chest and clasped her upper arms with her hands to ward off the lost, alone feeling.

Her dark eyes unconsciously followed Christian as he prowled about the large, high-ceilinged room, his hands thrust in the back pockets of his jeans. A dark scowl masked his features. In spite of herself, Toni couldn't help but smile.

"My aunt usually watches one of her favorite westerns at this time. Are you fond of cowboys and Indians?"

Christian stopped his aimless pacing and stared straight into her eyes. "I'm *fond* of you, Antonia. So put your formal manners away and sit down. Believe it or not, I'm not going to attack you," he said huskily.

"I never for a moment thought you would, Christian," she said, trying to defend herself.

"Oh? Then perhaps you'll tell me why you react like a frightened rabbit each time I take you in my arms? We both know what the outcome is going to be."

For a moment Toni considered what he'd said, then asked, "Why haven't you ever married, Christian?"

"What kind of damn fool question is that?"

"A simple one, I should think. It seems highly unlikely that with all your experience over the years, you haven't met at least one woman who made you consider marriage."

He walked over and dropped down onto the sofa, then patted the cushion beside him. "May we sit during this examination of my wasted youth?"

"Of course." Toni smiled, feeling much more confident now that he was on the defensive. She sat down with one foot drawn beneath her and faced him. "Are you going to answer my question?"

"I'd rather kiss you than talk," he said engagingly, one hand snaking out to glide along her thigh.

"Stop that!" Toni said sternly, her only recourse being to catch his wandering hand in her own and hold it.

"Well, at least you're touching me without my having to resort to stronger methods."

Toni ignored the taunt. "I'm waiting." She smiled sweetly at him.

He sighed. "So you are. I'm afraid you'll be disappointed, sweetheart, for there's nothing dark and wicked to reveal. As I said once before, there have been one or two women in the past who have caused me to give fleeting thought to marriage, but it was *only* a thought, and *so* fleeting that I can barely remember their faces."

"I don't believe you," Toni snapped.

"Why? Have I shot a hole in the elaborate tale you were planning to regale me with?" An amused yet tender expression swept over his face.

"It's not so elaborate, I'm afraid, and it's not a tale." She looked down at their hands, their fingers laced together. "Right now I'm about as confused as a woman can be."

"May I make a suggestion?"

"Yes."

"Stop analyzing each thing that happens between us, honey." He reached for her other hand. "I'm aware that our af—" He smiled. "Sorry . . . our relationship has been moving along with the speed of a jet. Quite frankly, I'm almost as amazed as you. But unlike you I'm not frightened. I like the experience."

"The words sound good," Toni said. She met his gaze squarely. "But can't we slow it down? I've already made one bad choice in my life. And even though what we have is somewhat different, I don't want to keep on making one mistake after another."

"Don't ever compare me with Steven Crowell, Antonia," Christian lashed out at her in a cold, harsh voice. "I may be some sort of low-life in your eyes, but I've never struck a woman nor have I ever put my ring on a woman's finger and forgot it when it suited me."

"Please . . ." Toni leaned toward him till her forehead was pressing against his cheek. "I didn't mean that you were like Steven."

And though the scowl remained on his face, his arms were quick to find their way around her waist and bring her fully against him. He lifted his head and watched her through narrowed lids. "I think I could forgive you for almost anything in the world when you're in my arms."

"Almost anything?" Toni asked as the fingers of one hand teased the dark hair revealed by the opening of his shirt. "What heinous crime would I have to commit that would deny me your forgiveness?"

"Sleeping with another man."

"Oh, dear." She sighed in mock despair. "Now you've gone and messed up my way of earning an extra income."

Before she could blink an eye, Toni found herself face down across Christian's lap, with one of his huge hands suspended over her behind. "You wouldn't dare!" she exclaimed breathlessly. "You just said you would never strike a woman."

"Correction, you little flirt," he growled. "I said I *had never* hit a woman. That was before I met you. I would also like to point out here and now that I don't care for the kind of joke you just made. Do I make myself clear?" he asked silkily.

"Hell yes, you overgrown oaf. What else do you expect me to say with all my blood rushing to my head?"

Just as quickly as Christian had turned her over his knee, he hoisted her back onto the sofa. Only this time there was one arm behind her shoulders and another in front at her waist. "Now," Christian said, smiling. "Do we understand each other better?"

"But of course." Toni returned his smile with an icy one of her own. "Considering that you have me locked in a near half nelson.

"Tsk, tsk. I'm always turned on by a submissive woman."

"Why, you—"

"Dinner is served," came Mrs. D's voice from the doorway.

Toni threw a startled glance toward the smiling housekeeper, a brilliant red staining her cheeks as she wondered just how much Mrs. D had seen and heard.

CHAPTER NINE

"Fishing?" Susie cried in disgust. "I can't believe I'm hearing correctly. Why on earth would you want to sit on a creek bank and mess with those awful wiggling worms when you could be having lunch in a nice restaurant?"

"Because Christian asked me to go with him," Toni told her, knowing quite well that the identity of her escort would put an end to her cousin's outcry.

"Oh. Well . . . in that case of course you have to accept. Can the two of you come over for dinner tomorrow evening? It'll be the first time I've been brave enough to have you both at the same time."

"Tomorrow sounds fine," Toni answered with a laugh. "But let me check with Christian to make sure. I'll call you when we get back this afternoon. Okay? I have to go now, Susie."

"Have fun, if that's possible."

Toni replaced the receiver and turned to find Christian standing impatiently just inside the kitchen. In one hand was the picnic basket Mrs. D had packed, and in the other was a red and black plaid blanket.

"Is your cousin trying to sabotage our outing?" he asked with brows arched as he hurried Toni out of the house and to his car.

"How did you guess?" She chuckled.

"Because Susie is about as restful to be around as a bee in a bed of spring flowers. If she were my wife I'd probably choke her."

"Susie is . . . meddlesome," Toni agreed. "But she means well."

Christian offered no comment and Toni really wasn't expecting one. She relaxed against the plush seat of the car and idly watched the scenery fly by. This was the second day in a row she'd spent with Christian.

The day before, they'd gone to New Orleans. They'd ridden the streetcar along St. Charles, taken the walking tour of the historic French Quarter, and eaten *beignets* at the old Café du Monde. They watched the artists at work in Jackson Square and then browsed through numerous antique shops. After a leisurely dinner in the early evening, they drove back to Natchez.

What had impressed Toni most of all about the day had been Christian's attitude. His attention hadn't faded in the least. If anything, it had intensified. And her own reaction to him was a pleasant surprise too. She felt none of the tension that always seemed to inhibit her around him. She found herself relaxing, and seeing for the first time the warm, gentle man beneath Christian's playboy façade.

On their return to Cartlaigne, however, her new-found confidence had been momentarily shaken when Christian insisted she come in for a drink.

On seeing her hesitation and the insecurity in her eyes, he had been quick to say, "Only a drink, Antonia. The next time I make love to you it will be because you want it."

And a drink was all it had been, accompanied by two hours or so of intimate conversation. It had been well past midnight when Christian had walked her to the cottage.

His good night kiss had sent shivers of excitement sweeping over her body and had her clinging to his shoulders for support. He caught her hands in his and held them. "I've never known a person determined to bring so much pain and suffering on herself as you," he said as he studied her face.

Her relationship with Christian may have been stormy, but her dreams that night had been peaceful and serene. She was with Christian on a deserted island so beautiful that it took her breath away. There seemed to be no distinction between night and day as they wandered their tropical paradise arm in arm. It was just the two of them, making love amid tropical splendor with the sound of a waterfall in the background.

Now, she was with him again. And though her imaginary island had quickly faded from her memory, she could still feel the touch of his hands running over the skin of her stomach to cup the fullness of her breasts. Her nipples hardened to tight, tiny points of desire as she remembered the hot caress of his tongue and the gentle sucking of his lips.

"According to Brent's directions, this should be the

place," came a faraway voice, intruding on the erotic thoughts swirling through her mind.

"Mmmmm," Toni murmured softly, unaware that the car had come to a halt.

"Having pleasant daydreams, Antonia?" a husky voice whispered against her ear as a large hand gently cupped the softness of one breast.

And though the spell of her dream had been shattered, she felt herself pressing against the hand at her breast as a wanton finger slowly, teasingly circled the burning tip.

She opened her eyes and stared into Christian's before making a half-hearted attempt to pull back. He easily stopped her, his hand slipping behind her to block the move. "Don't be embarrassed, sweetheart. I assure you, the feeling is mutual."

His lips took possession of hers with electrifying swiftness, and Toni knew in an instant that there would be no resistance on her part if he chose to make love to her. When his tongue demanded entrance to the hot moistness of her mouth, her lips parted willingly.

A giant shudder hit her like a tidal wave as their tongues met and became locked in an erotic skirmish that sent shock after shock trembling through her body.

Reluctantly, Christian drew back far enough to stare into her face. "My God!" he muttered hoarsely. "I honestly think I'm going out of my mind."

Toni raised tentative fingers and caressed the granite line of his jaw. "Welcome to the club. I've been suffering from a similar malaise for days now."

"You do know what will happen if we don't get the

hell out of this car, don't you?" he asked, his mouth a rigidly controlled line.

"Ah, but according to my cousin, the thought of catching a big-mouth bass is supposed to be paramount in a man's mind on outings of this sort."

"I've hinted at it before, but this time I'll be specific. Your cousin is a very silly but likable woman. And the term is large-mouth bass, not big mouth."

"Big-mouth, large-mouth . . . what's the difference?" Toni grinned. "Are you going to sit here all day idling away our time or are you going to catch my supper?"

"Only if we share."

"I'll definitely give it some thought," she said easily, the glow from his kiss still lingering in her eyes.

Careful to insure her comfort while he fished, Christian settled Toni beneath a large tree with spreading branches. "I think I'll start over there," he said, pointing to an area where several cypress trees dotted the surface of the water, "and work my way back here."

"Good luck." Toni smiled at him. She sat down with her back resting against the tree and opened the paperback mystery she'd bought the day before in New Orleans.

It was one of those fall days in the South when the mercury dropped to near freezing at night, only to rise to sixty or sixty-five during the day. The sun was shining brightly, and after an hour or so of reading, Toni's eyelids began to droop. Soon she was fast asleep, the book falling from her hands to the blanket.

Christian's solitary figure slowly made its way around the bank, a look of satisfaction on his tanned face as the number of his catch steadily increased.

It was the rustle of paper and the sharp pop of a

canned drink being snapped opened that roused Toni from her slumber. She opened her eyes, squinting against the brightness of the sun, and saw Christian sitting beside her, calmly setting out the food.

"What time is it?" she asked after a huge stretch and a jaw-cracking yawn.

"Almost one thirty." He smiled at her. "You were sleeping so peacefully I didn't have the heart to disturb you."

"Thanks. But now that I am awake, I'm starving." She took a deep breath of the fresh air and shook her head. "If I did this regularly, I'm afraid I'd be as round as I am tall. The outdoors gives me a terrific appetite."

"In that case, I'll have to limit our nature treks to only once a month," Christian said firmly. He handed her a plate piled with fried chicken, potato salad, tiny cucumber sandwiches, and deviled eggs.

"Ha! Look who's talking," she scoffed, eyeing the same food on his plate, the amount of each selection doubled.

"But the difference is, my black-eyed minx, I've been working," he responded in true male fashion.

"I saw." Toni pulled a long face. "One step every five minutes. That isn't the sort of exercise that burns up the enormous amount of calories you're consuming."

"You're a mean-hearted shrew."

"True," she said with a laugh, "but a truthful one. By the way, how was your luck?"

"I have five very nice bass, Miss Know-it-all. Doesn't it make you feel bad, knowing that while you were snoring under this tree, I was slaving away to provide your supper?"

"Not at all," Toni returned as she bit into a golden-brown chicken breast. "However, I'm sure you'll come up with something to get back at me."

The harmless banter continued throughout the meal, and Toni became more and more relaxed. Christian had made no move to touch her, apparently content with one firm thigh resting against hers while they ate.

When they'd polished off the last crumb of food, Christian moved their plates and empty cans aside, then stretched out on his back. It seemed the most natural thing in the world for him to reach out and pull Toni down beside him.

"I never knew fishing could be so enjoyable," she teased lazily as she wiggled around till her cheek was resting on his shoulder. Without thinking, she slipped one hand beneath the front of his shirt, her fingers absently toying with the crisp dark hair on his chest.

"It isn't with everyone." Christian turned his head so that their faces were only inches apart. "As a matter of fact, picnics and fishing trips are two more items I'll have to add to that list of things you aren't allowed to do with other men."

"Mmmm . . . what else is on this list?" she murmured huskily, the feel of his warm skin beneath the sensitive tips of her fingers filling her with a tingling excitement.

"Well, of course you aren't allowed to go out with other men," he breathed against her cheek. "And that first rule sort of takes care of the second one, which is that if you ever went to bed with another man, I'd wring your beautiful little neck."

"Sounds terrifying." She strained closer and nipped the tip of his earlobe with her teeth. "Haven't you learned by now that we Cartlaigne women resent being told what to do?"

For several intense seconds Christian was silent as he watched her. "What I'm learning at the moment, Antonia, is that you are, either unwittingly or deliberately, setting out to seduce me. Would you care to tell me which it is?"

The pink tip of Toni's tongue ran hurriedly over lips that had gone dry as she pondered his question. He was painfully and embarrassingly correct. Call it seduction or just plain need, it made no difference. What did matter, though, was the hunger gnawing inside her for this man. He'd said he wouldn't force her till she wanted him. Well, she reminded herself, she'd learned that the only way to get what you really wanted was to reach out and take it.

"I've never made love on a blanket beneath a tree," she said, so quietly that Christian could barely hear her. But words were unnecessary, for nothing on earth could disguise the invitation in her eyes or the soft, pliant shape of her slender body pressed against him.

With unhurried ease their fingers began to loosen buttons and zippers. As each article of clothing was removed it was replaced by hands that glided and smoothed their way inch by inch to the next barrier.

It wasn't only Christian who kissed and touched his way over pink-tipped breasts and satiny thighs. Newly confident, Toni became aggressive in her quest to know the secrets of this tanned body that held such tremendous power over her.

Her small hands ran lazily over his broad shoulders and muscled back, feeling the controlled strength beneath her touch. She continued her exploration until her fingers lightly feathered the leanness of his hips and buttocks. At that point she became hesitant, unsure.

"Touch me, Antonia. Don't be afraid." Christian's voice floated against her ear. "I enjoy the feel of your hands on my body as much as you enjoy having me caress you."

"I'm not very experienced at this sort of thing," she murmured, her body going taut with desire as his urgent lips caught and pulled at the tip of her breast.

"Stop worrying about technique, honey, and do what your heart tells you," he rasped as the tip of his hot tongue made teasing circles on the satiny mound of her breast.

With his words of encouragement to guide her, Toni ran her hands lovingly over his buttocks and the hardness of his thighs, glorying in her moment of triumph when she felt his muscles stiffen, his breathing become harsh and ragged.

She delighted in the exploration of his body and wantonly urged Christian on to even more intimate investigations of hers. By the time he had begun to tenderly feather kisses across her stomach and the tense softness of her inner thighs, she was screaming inside with the need to be taken, to be possessed.

"I said I wouldn't make love to you again until you decided you wanted me," Christian whispered, settling his body above hers and staring intently into her dark, burning eyes. "Do you want me, Antonia?"

"Oh, yes!" she answered in a wild rush, her hands grasping his shoulders to force him closer. Her head was thrashing from side to side, her black hair shining like a velvet cloud. "I want you . . . I need you . . ."

Then and only then did she feel the first roughness

of his knee between hers and felt their bodies coming together to fulfill their intense desire.

He entered her waiting softness, and Toni heard herself crying out his name in unashamed abandon. Strong but gentle arms surrounded her as the passion that possessed each of them pushed them closer and closer to ultimate release. Only the whispered sounds escaping them and their labored breathing disturbed the sleepy cove sheltered by the huge, spreading oak.

"Happy?" Christian smiled down at her as he drove with one hand, his other arm keeping Toni a willing prisoner against his side.

"Happy," she said without hesitation, wanting this moment, this sense of well-being, to last forever.

"We're almost home. When we get there, are you going to remain as sweet and loving as you've been these last two days, or are you going to turn back into that disagreeable female I've been forced to deal with?"

"I really can't say, Christian," she said innocently, mischief dancing in her eyes. "We females are notorious for our chameleon-like moods. I think . . . I'll probably not get the urge to murder you for at least another day or two, but alas"—she shrugged dramatically—"who can say?"

"Spoken like the little witch you are," he answered with a frown. "Before you start feeling so proud of yourself though, Miss Grant, I'd like to remind you that I do have ways of taming that wicked tongue of yours."

Toni glared at him. "Why do I waste my time with you, you arrogant toad?" She turned her head and stared straight ahead, her chin lifted defiantly. "I think I'll call Raymond. Even listening to his stories about his dogs is more pleasant than being a constant source of nourishment for your ego."

"Let's see now . . . which one is he?" Christian grinned evilly.

"The one who wanted to take me for a walk in the fog," Toni informed him, struggling to keep from giggling. "You frightened the living daylights out of him when you came crashing through the bushes when he kissed me."

"Ah well, if you insist on settling for second best, I suppose he's as good as any. But when you're ready to go first class again, you can always whistle."

"Why, you egotistical fool!" Toni exclaimed, then retaliated by pinching him just above the waist.

"Ouch! That hurt!" he bellowed, trying to dodge her quick fingers before she could dish out further pain and punishment.

"I meant it to, you swine," she said sweetly. "Whistle indeed . . . you should live so long."

"All right, all right," a laughing Christian shouted. "I'm sorry . . . I'll eat only bread and water for days. And you won't have to whistle, I'll do it. Okay?"

"I'll think about it," Toni muttered, doing her best to act uninterested.

Christian turned into the drive at Cartlaigne, still chuckling. "If I promise to behave, will you go fishing with me tomorrow?" he whispered in her ear.

"That depends," she answered slowly, her gaze resting on the strange car in the drive beside the cottage. "Mrs. D didn't mention anything about having company today. I wonder if Aunt Sara's gotten worse."

"I'm sure someone would have come and gotten us

if that were the case. Perhaps it's your friend from Richmond."

"Steven?" Toni asked, her heart sinking.

"There's only one way to find out," Christian answered shortly, his happy, relaxed mood evaporating. He drove to the garage behind the big house, switched off the engine, then turned to Toni. "If it is Crowell, I want your word you won't see him alone."

"Don't you think you're being a little bit ridiculous? After all, we can hardly talk with Mrs. D hovering in the background like a watchful duenna," she protested.

"Your word, Toni." His voice was as cold as the steely points of his eyes. "He almost took a swing at you the last time you were together, and I don't know what he might try if you don't say what he wants to hear. I think you know what I'd do if he touched you, don't you?"

Toni cleared her throat nervously and slowly nodded. "Yes, I know, Christian, and I appreciate your concern. But surely he wouldn't be foolish enough to try something like that."

At least I hope he wouldn't, she thought, *because Christian will murder him. Maybe it isn't Steven at all,* she hoped. *Perhaps he's had time to reconsider since he called.*

But any such hope on Toni's part was quickly dashed when she and Christian entered the kitchen and found Mrs. D in a classic dither.

"Oh, my, Toni," the older woman said anxiously. "I'm so glad to see you." She cast an apprehensive glance toward Christian, then went on. "Steven Crowell is in the sitting room. He's been here for almost two hours. I'm afraid I haven't been as gracious to that young man as I should have been, but considering the circumstances, I don't feel very hospitable toward him."

Toni smiled and gave the housekeeper a sympathetic pat on the shoulder. "You're not to worry. I'm sure that once Steven and I talk, he'll be on his way back to Richmond."

She turned to Christian, who was leaning against the counter, his massive arms crossed over his broad chest, a murderous gleam in his blue eyes. The sleeves of his blue checked shirt were rolled back to reveal strong forearms, and the faded jeans clung to his muscled thighs like a second skin.

"There's really no need for you to stay, you know," she said softly.

"I'm not leaving, Antonia, so why don't you go on in and talk with Crowell, then send him on his way. I'll have a cup of Mrs. D's coffee and keep her company."

And keep me terrified, knowing you're hovering in the background, Toni wanted to add, but didn't. She'd long since learned just how stubborn Christian could be. She was also well aware of exactly what he thought of Steven. She wanted to avoid another confrontation between the two men if at all possible.

"Very well." She smiled, then turned and made her way to the sitting room.

Steven, who was sitting on the sofa, bounded to his feet and raced across the room toward her the moment Toni entered.

"Toni!" he exclaimed, reaching out and clasping her in a warm embrace before she could stop him.

"Hello, Steven," she replied coolly, firmly extricating herself from his arms before he had a chance to kiss her.

She stationed herself behind a high-backed chair, almost laughing at the crestfallen expression that clouded Steven's face at her open rejection.

"I'm sorry you've been kept waiting. But since you didn't give me any idea of when you'd be arriving . . ."

"No problem," he offered expansively. "Although that dragon of a housekeeper hasn't been especially pleasant."

"Ah, yes, Mrs. D." Toni chuckled. "I'm afraid you'll have to forgive her, Steven. You see, she's been here since before I was born. She also knows what happened between us and doesn't feel at all charitable toward you. By the way, how is Lea?"

At the mention of the other woman's name, Steven had the grace to blush. He ran a forefinger around the crisp collar of his white shirt in a clearly nervous gesture. "Fine, I suppose. Actually I haven't seen her in several weeks. But I didn't come here to talk about Lea," he said with determination. "I want to talk about us . . . you and me, Toni. Now that we've had time to get over our little tiff, I'm sure we can work things out."

"It wasn't a little tiff, Steven," she calmly corrected him, keeping a tight clamp on her rising temper. "And there isn't anything to work out. I tried to tell you that when you called earlier in the week."

"I'm afraid I can't accept that, sweetheart," he said, smiling confidently. He walked to the front of the chair she was standing behind and placed his neat, manicured fingers on the brocaded back. "You're still angry with me and . . ." He tipped his head engagingly. "I understand. But I'm not leaving here until my ring is back on your finger."

"Then I hope you're looking forward to retiring in this area, Steven. I don't want your ring back," she told him firmly and without hesitation, wondering, as she did, how she could ever have thought herself in love with this insufferable man.

"That's what you say now, but after we've spent some time together, I'm sure you'll feel differently. Let's start by having dinner this evening."

"Dinner's out of the question, Crowell," said Christian from the doorway. "Antonia and I have plans for this evening."

At the first sound of Christian's voice, Toni and Steven turned and stared at him in surprise. There was a look of utter astonishment on Steven's face. His mouth, opened wide in amazement, reminded Toni of one of the fish waiting outside to be cleaned.

His expression quickly changed to one of suspicious belligerence. "What are you doing here?" he asked angrily.

Christian strolled lazily into the room, not stopping until he was standing beside Toni. With a practiced ease that caused Steven's eyes to narrow, he slipped an arm around Toni's waist.

"You could say I live here, or rather, next door. I've leased Cartlaigne for six months."

"Why didn't you tell me this before?" Steven turned accusing eyes on Toni. "Is he the reason you're being so stubborn about everything?"

"I didn't tell you about Christian living next door, Steven, because frankly I didn't see how it concerned you. As for your last question, don't you think we've discussed that issue enough?"

"I won't stop until you come to your senses," he threw out challengingly. "I'm staying at the Ramada on the bluff." He turned and walked to the door, then paused. "I'll call you later, when we can talk without being interrupted."

He stomped loudly down the hall and slammed the front door with a resounding bang. Moments later Toni heard a car flinging gravel as it sped down the half-mile drive to the blacktop.

"I don't think your friend Steven has learned to control his temper at all, do you, Antonia?" Christian asked against the deafening silence hanging over the room.

"In all fairness, his anger didn't surface until you entered the picture," she pointed out. "Which is also rather surprising. I never realized Steven was jealous."

Christian turned her around to face him, his arms completely shackling her to him. "Since I'm sure you took your engagement to him very seriously he probably didn't have cause to be jealous. But that's over. Now there's someone else in your life and I won't allow the likes of Steven Crowell to intimidate my woman."

"Aren't you being rather bossy, Mr. Barr? And possessive?" Toni grinned up at him. "I don't recall you asking *your woman* what she thinks about you deciding if and when she can see another man."

"I think, Miss Grant," he said in a tone of voice Toni had difficulty defining, "that permission, along with several other things, was given to me today by that *certain woman* on a blanket beside a lake."

Whether or not she could have convinced Steven the next day that there could never be a reconciliation between them, Toni wasn't to know. For during the night, in the early hours before dawn, she was awakened by Mrs. D and told that her aunt had quietly died in her sleep.

The next couple of days seemed to stretch interminably for Toni and Susie as they prepared for their aunt's funeral.

Creighton Samuels, Jr., of the law firm of Samuels, Samuels, and Clark, had given Toni and Susie a sympathetic grin when he told them of their aunt's instructions concerning her own funeral. She had demanded that it be held privately with a minimum of fuss, as soon as possible after her death. "Even in death Miss Sara was determined to have her way," he told them solemnly.

"I wouldn't be surprised to actually hear her reprimand us if we don't carry on exactly as she's instructed," Toni remarked. She turned and reached for the fresh pot of coffee Mrs. D had made. "More coffee, Creighton? Susie?"

At a nod from each, she refilled their cups and her own, then leaned back in her chair. Creighton was an old and good friend. Both Toni and Susie had dated him in high school. He joined his father's firm directly out of law school. Oddly enough, something about his blond, boyish appearance had pleased Sara Cartlaigne. Shortly after he became associated with the firm, she changed from Creighton senior to his son.

"This is one time I'd like to go against her wishes," Toni said with a sigh. "I feel like some sort of monster burying her so quickly."

"I agree," Susie said softly. "But to be quite honest, Toni, I'd be afraid not to. Lightning might strike us if we didn't follow her instructions to the letter."

The funeral was just as Sara Cartlaigne had wanted. Afterward the reading of the will took place in the small, seldom used library at the cottage.

Mrs. D was taken care of for life. Sara also asked that Toni allow the housekeeper to make her home at the cottage if the older woman so desired.

The Cartlaigne jewelry was left equally to Toni and Susie, as was Sara's money. But it was a surprise to everyone that Aunt Sara had willed the cottage to Toni.

Now, for the first time, an unmarried Cartlaigne female had been given the right to sell the property. It had also been Sara's choice that Toni be her heir to the antiques and the few acres making up the small estate.

CHAPTER TEN

Toni sat across the table from Steven, barely able to contain herself as the meal drew to a close. Some ridiculous sense of loyalty had prompted her to accept his invitation, that and the kindness he'd shown since her aunt died. Since Christian was away for the day, there didn't seem any harm in having lunch with her ex-fiancé.

"This has been like old times," Steven said, smiling as he drank the last of his coffee. "I can't tell you how much I've missed you, Toni."

"Please, Steven," she said, trying to stop him. "You promised not to bring up that subject."

"Okay." He quickly raised both hands in a conciliatory gesture. "I'm sorry. I won't mention it again today. If you're ready, I'll take you home. I think I'll spend the rest of the afternoon touring some of the old homes."

As they approached Cartlaigne and its imposing façade, Steven stared thoughtfully at the beautiful old place. "Does it make you sad that it's no longer in your family?"

"Heavens no!" Toni exclaimed. "The cottage is trouble enough without having the backbreaking job of maintaining the big house as well. No," she said firmly, "even though I want to see it remain in caring hands, I have no desire to be responsible for it. Besides, this is the place I've always loved." She waved one hand toward the cottage. "To me this has always been the real Cartlaigne. I suppose that's because Aunt Sara was always there. Aunt Sara *was* Cartlaigne."

"Will you stay here?"

"For a while. After that . . . who knows?"

"Can I see you tomorrow morning?" Steven asked. "I'm afraid I have to get back to Richmond. But I will be returning to Natchez, Toni. Your aunt's death has been a shock to you and I don't want to press you. But I know there is a future for us. And after you've had time to think about it, so will you."

Rather than argue with him, an exercise she'd already found to be a waste of breath, she asked, "What time does your plane leave?"

"Eleven fifty-five."

"Until tomorrow then." Toni smiled and reached out to open the door.

But Steven wasn't to be put off so easily. He leaned over and cupped the back of her head, his other hand gripping her arm. "How about a kiss?" he murmured huskily.

And during that brief moment when Toni was staring at him as though he'd gone crazy, Steven lost no time in claiming her lips. It was the second time he'd tried to kiss her since his arrival in Natchez. And now, as with the first time, the only emotion he evoked in her was an overwhelming urgency to remove herself from his touch.

She squirmed away from him and quickly got out of the car. Once she was safe, with the door securely closed behind her, she gave Steven a weak smile, a brief wave of one hand, then turned and sought the security of the cottage.

When she entered the house and closed the door, she saw Mrs. D and Susie peering out the window at Steven's car as it disappeared down the driveway.

"I'm certainly glad Christian wasn't here to see that tender embrace," Susie teased, not the least perturbed at being caught spying on her cousin. Neither, for that matter, was the housekeeper.

"Is he paying the two of you to watch me?" Toni asked sweetly, the expression in her dark eyes belying the friendly tone of her voice.

"Don't be so testy, Antonia." Susie chuckled. "Mrs. D and I have never been so nicely entertained. Though I must admit, being fairly certain of the outcome does make for more pleasant watching."

"Has anyone ever told you that you are a busybody, Susie?" Toni asked with a frown. She stared at each of her tormentors, then shrugged. "You're both terrible."

"I think we've teased her enough, Susie." Mrs. D smiled, speaking for the first time. "Why don't I make a pot of coffee? We still have several boxes and two trunks left to go through."

The remainder of the afternoon was spent as the two previous ones had been, sorting and going through Sara's belongings. When they finished, Toni left the room rather hurriedly, her head throbbing from the sharp odor of mothballs.

"I hope I never smell that odor again," she said as she collapsed in a chair at the table in the kitchen.

"My sentiments exactly," Susie muttered as she reached for her jacket and purse.

"Don't you have time for a quick cup of coffee?" Mrs. D asked.

"I'd love it," Susie said, "but I have to fix dinner. The two of you can get by with a bowl of soup and a sandwich. I have to cook in order to fill the cavernous stomachs of my family."

"How sad," Toni replied in mock sympathy. "You know very well you could give Brent a plate of straw and he wouldn't complain."

"Perhaps." Her carefree cousin shrugged. "But every now and then I just love playing the poor overworked housewife."

When they were finally alone, the housekeeper and Toni enjoyed one of their long talks. Toni had always felt close to the older woman. For as long as she could remember, Mrs. D had been a part of Cartlaigne, her presence felt in every corner. She also loved the housekeeper because of her closeness with her aunt. Both women were adrift without Sara, each reaching out to the other to fill the void left by the old woman's death.

"I haven't asked, Mrs. D, but do you want to remain here?" Toni asked.

"Yes," the elderly woman said with a nod. "I've no family except for a sister. She has a son, and even though they are always glad to see me, I feel as though I'd be intruding in their lives. But what about you, Toni? Are you going to leave an old woman to knock around all these empty rooms by herself or will you make this your home?"

"It gets more difficult each day to even think of

leaving. So," she said, smiling at Mrs. D, "there'll probably be two of us knocking around. Although, for the life of me, I can't figure out what kind of job I can get in this town."

"Now, don't you fret." Mrs. D patted her hand consolingly. "With the money Sara left us, we have quite a while before we have to worry about starving."

Toni smiled, then looked thoughtfully at her friend. "It's still hard for me to accept the idea of my aunt Sara wheeling and dealing in the stock market."

"Your aunt was born way before her time, honey. I've often thought she'd have been able to run any large corporation as well or better than most men. She could even have gone into politics. A woman like Sara could have been governor or a congresswoman. She could charm the birds out of the trees when it suited her, or be hard as nails."

Later, as Toni showered to remove the mothball smell from her skin and hair, then dressed in a pair of emerald-green slacks and a matching sweater, she wondered if she had been wise to get Mrs. D's hopes up by saying she planned to stay in Natchez. For in all honesty, she wasn't sure what she wanted to do.

Since her affair with Christian had begun, there hadn't been room enough in her thoughts for unexciting things such as jobs and what she should do to support herself. In spite of her determination not to make more of their relationship than there really was, Toni found herself doing just that. It was so easy to sit and wonder what it would be like to have his children, but it was also very easy to wonder how long he would be content to come home to the same woman.

Hadn't he told her there'd always been an understanding with the women he became involved with? No commitment, no ties, had been his motto.

Then why the various displays of jealousy he'd shown, first with the men Susie paraded beneath his nose, then his outright anger when Steven called? The actual arrival of her former fiancé had turned that anger to cold, hard rage and had Christian watching her every step.

Did that sound like a man interested only in a brief affair? she wondered.

"But what about me?" she whispered. "I turned to Steven at a time in my life when I was most vulnerable. Is that what I'm doing with Christian? Am I unconsciously attempting to create, to manipulate innocently spoken words into what I want to hear and believe?"

What exactly do I want, she wondered. *Have I finally accepted Susie's idea that real happiness can only be found in marriage? Do I care enough for Christian to marry him? Would he ever even ask me.* She grimaced.

Oh, yes, she answered her own question. *You care enough for him. You love him enough to follow him to hell and back.*

"Maybe it's time for me to pick myself up and stop worrying and wondering about what Christian's going to do next," she said aloud. "Somehow the idea of sitting around waiting for a man to decide whether or not he wants me isn't very appealing. Besides," she said, grinning at her reflection in the mirror, "I just might decide I *don't want* Mr. Barr. I wonder what he'd do then."

"I hope you don't mind my holding back dinner for a few minutes, Toni," Mrs. D said with an excited lilt in her voice as she scurried about the kitchen. "I invited Christian to eat with us and he should be here any minute now."

"Not at all, Mrs. D." Toni thoughtfully tilted her head to one side, wondering just when these plans had been made. "Did he say where he was going today?"

"I believe he mentioned New Orleans. Something to do with an article he wants to do on the rising crime rate in the French Quarter."

Toni smothered her amusement at the housekeeper's perfect recital of what Christian had told her. At that moment the back door burst open and the tardy dinner guest swept into the kitchen, carrying two large bags of groceries.

"Hello, ladies." Christian smiled broadly, his gaze sweeping over Toni and lingering on the firm set of her lips. "Mrs. D, I brought you some French bread, some wine, and a few other little goodies," he told the beaming housekeeper as he set the bags on the counter. "Give me a few minutes to wash up and I'll be ready for that gumbo you promised me."

Dinner was delicious, or so Christian kept telling Mrs. D. Toni would have been just as happy eating hay as she was the thick, dark shrimp gumbo served over a bed of fluffy rice.

Each time she risked a glance toward Christian, she found him watching her. The dancing glow of his eyes seemed somehow sensuous and exciting. It was almost as though he were actually touching her.

By the time they finished dessert, Toni had begun to wonder if Christian had slipped some mysterious mind-numbing drug into her food. But she knew better. At some point within the last few days she'd come full circle with her feelings for him.

Perhaps it was Steven, with his untimely visit and his attempts to push his way back into her life, that had caused it. It was impossible for Toni not to compare the two men, she told herself as Christian and Mrs. D talked.

Steven was a worm, as she'd learned to her sorrow. He had no conception of love; all he understood were his own wants and needs. Hers didn't seem to matter. Christian, however, offered her a totally different type of relationship. He was strong and determined, but sensitive to her needs and desires. Their lovemaking was the joining together of two halves into a perfect oneness . . . a whole and complete unit.

Sometime later a rather subdued Toni walked beside Christian toward the big house. "You've changed from a bewitching seductress to a very quiet young woman during the last hour, Antonia. Why?" Christian asked as he unlocked the door and held it open for her.

"One can't stay *up* continuously," she said quietly, making her way to the warm fire that was burning in the fireplace.

Christian shrugged off his jacket and dropped it onto a chair, his hooded gaze sweeping over her. There was guarded caution in his expressive features as he studied the tense set of her shoulders.

"I don't think it's a simple matter of ups and downs that's bothering you, honey," he said matter-of-factly. He walked over and stood at one side of the fireplace, an elbow propped on the mantel. "Is it our relationship that's the problem?"

Toni lifted her gaze from the dancing flames and stared at him, then looked away. What she was feeling was too new, too private to share with him yet. Especially when she knew so well that commitment wasn't a possibility.

"What you're really asking is whether or not I'm beginning to think of you as a part of my future, aren't you? Well, don't worry, Christian. I have no long-range plans that include you." She forced herself to smile. "Your record will remain unblemished."

Christian tipped his dark head, bringing his stubborn chin to rest on his fist. "What would you say if I were to tell you that I'm ready to relinquish my title? That I resent not being included in your future?"

The sudden acceleration of her heartbeat was so severe that Toni was positive Christian could hear it. She swallowed against the surge of excitement threatening to choke her. *Calm down,* she sternly lectured herself. *He's probably gone through this particular little scene countless times.*

"I'd think you were an accomplished actor and not be overly concerned. Once the realization of what you'd done hit you, you'd find some way to back out gracefully."

Christian frowned. "I never knew you had such a low opinion of me, Antonia."

"That's not so, Christian," she protested. "You're one of the most honest men I've ever known."

"Honest?" he repeated. "You really think I'm honest?"

"Yes, I do."

"I wonder what you really think of me," he murmured softly, a tender smile smoothing his lips. "Do you approve of my type of journalism?"

"I think you try to present all sides of the story," Toni said frankly.

"Do you think I'm what the ladies could call handsome?" he asked cockily.

"No," she answered without hesitation. "Your features are too rugged and your nose is a mess."

"Mmm," he muttered consideringly. "How about my taste in food, the way I dress, my favorite hobby. Oh, and don't forget the charming way I treat a woman. What's your opinion of the above?"

Toni stared at him as though he'd lost his mind. She shook her head and then turned and walked the few steps to the sofa and sat down. "Are you thinking of compiling a resumé to send out to all the available women you know?"

"A resumé!" He gave every appearance of being enthralled with the idea. "Would you help me work out the details?" he asked innocently as he joined her on the sofa.

"I will not," she replied sharply, her dark eyes shooting sparks.

"Don't make such a hasty decision, Antonia. We'd change the wording a bit, perhaps play up my physical attributes, even enhance, on paper of course, my *rugged* features and my nose which is a *mess.* The possibilities are limitless."

"Need I tell you what you can do with your physical attributes, your rugged features, and your messy nose?" Toni eyed him distastefully.

Christian shook his head slowly, his expression somber. One long arm snaked out and settled over her shoulder. Toni started to move to the edge of the cushion, when he suddenly opened his hand and let a small dark box drop into her lap.

"You drive a hard bargain, Antonia. Will this make you feel a little kinder toward me?"

She picked up the velvet-covered case, her heart sinking as she opened and stared at the beautiful diamond inside. Feel kindly toward him? she asked herself. How could she feel any kindness toward him when he was so cruel as to think a gift, even one as beautiful as the ring, was suitable *payment* for what they'd shared? How could she feel kindness toward him when he considered her such a shallow person as to be willing to accept such a payment? And how could he be so cruel as to offer a ring that was usually given as a symbol of betrothal?

"It's beautiful, Christian," she said quietly, then closed the lid and offered it back to him. "But I'm afraid it's a little too much, don't you? If you've been this generous with the other women in your life, I'm surprised that you've remained solvent."

Christian looked puzzled for a moment, then he had the nerve to throw back his head and roar with laughter. Toni remained sitting on the edge of the sofa, determined to keep control of her emotions if it killed her.

When he had himself under control, he stared at Toni quietly for a moment, his eyes warm and infinitely tender. He plucked the box from her hand, opened it, and removed the ring. "This, my suspicious-minded imp, whether you believe it or not, is an engagement ring." He reached for her left hand and slipped the ring on the appropriate finger.

"Why do you want to marry me?" Toni asked numbly.

"Because I love you." Christian smiled, bringing her hand to his lips and pressing a kiss to each of her fingers. "Because you are such a meek, obedient little thing," he said with dancing eyes. "Because *calmness* surrounds you, and I know our days together will pass without the slightest ripple of conflict." He paused, then asked, "How does that sound?"

"Like the conceited toad you are," she answered, struggling to keep a straight face. "But I think the real reason behind your offer is my inheritance."

"Oh, that definitely counts in your favor," he solemnly agreed. "Especially the goat and the rooster."

By this time Toni was beside herself with laughter. She threw herself into his waiting arms, tears of happiness slipping from her eyes and leaving glistening trails down her cheeks.

"I love you so much, Christian," she murmured, her lips finding their way to the skin of his neck. "And I will marry you," she whispered between soft, feathery kisses.

"My God!" he exclaimed, grasping her by the upper arms. "This is the first time you've agreed with me on anything. Are you sure you're feeling all right?"

"No." She smiled, her lashes wet with tears. "I'm sure I'm dreaming. Isn't there something you can do to help me separate reality from fantasy?"

"Gladly." Christian grinned, then brought a squeal of surprise to her lips by suddenly rising to his feet with her high in his arms and heading for the bedroom. "Having a wife who's no bigger than my fist is going to have its rewards," he whispered huskily, letting her slowly slide inch by inch down his body till her feet touched the floor. They were standing beside the bed, and Toni's knees began to tremble as she anticipated what was about to happen.

It was as though Christian were meting out a delightful brand of punishment, she thought several dazed moments later as she stood quietly before him. As each piece of clothing was removed from her body with unhurried ease, his hands, his lips, touched each bared portion of soft skin. Toni's thoughts became a helpless jumble of feelings and emotions. All she knew was that she wanted this man more intensely than she had ever wanted anything else.

When Christian picked her up and laid her on the bed, Toni closed her eyes against the aching fire within her, almost crying out for him to hurry. She was amazingly alert to the slightest noise he made as he undressed. Alert and ready to open her arms and her heart to him the very instant she felt the bed give and knew the feel of his hair-roughened thigh easing between her own smooth legs.

She arched toward the warmth of his large body, the tips of her breasts snuggling against the dark hair of his chest, the friction from the contact sending a huge shudder throughout her body.

Christian brought his hands to the sides of her breasts, his thumbs briskly circling and teasing the already stiff nipples. "I love you, Antonia," he whispered hoarsely as their bodies merged and became one in a rhythm of passion and fire as old as man.

Even though the morning was gray and overcast, inside the kitchen of the big house one would have thought the sun was shining full force . . . or so it seemed to the man and woman sitting at the table. And in spite of the constant bickering between bites of scrambled eggs and bacon, nothing could erase the love in Christian's eyes even as he emphasized his remarks by glaring fiercely at his intended across the table.

"I damn well have no intention of waiting six months before I marry you," he finished in a loud voice.

"You're an insensitive clod," Toni fired right back, reaching for her coffee and boldly staring at him over the rim of the cup. "Have you no respect at all for the dead?" she hissed as though afraid of someone overhearing her.

"I respected your aunt Sara very much, Antonia, and you know it. She'd also be the first to tell you not to be so stubborn," Christian countered. "You know exactly what she thought of a 'decent period' of mourning and all the other foolish notions you and Susie might come up with."

Toni sat back and regarded him stonily for several minutes. "I suppose you're right. But it will be a simple wedding, mind you. I have no desire to float down the aisle like a tugboat pulling a string of barges behind me. And that's what will happen if Susie has any say in the matter."

"I'll handle Susie," Christian reassured her soothingly. "We'll get our blood tests today and be married on Thursday. How does that sound?"

"Like I'm pregnant and someone is nudging you in the behind with a shotgun." She grinned, then a sobering expression suddenly flitted across her face. "Are you certain, Christian?" she asked. "This has all been so fast. I feel like I'm on a runaway train and there's nobody at the controls."

"Good." He smiled, then caught her hand in his warm grasp. "That's the way I want to keep you until you say 'I do.' "

"Fink!"

"In the flesh," he admitted unashamedly.

"I have no idea where you live," she said, trying to sound serious. "For all I know, you don't even have a house."

"I'll have you know, I have a very nice home in Virginia," he smugly replied, then gave her a sheepish grin. "At least I used to. I've always moved around quite a bit, so my sister sort of keeps an eye on it for me."

"Will there be a place for my goat and rooster at this home you 'think' you have?" she teased.

Christian was about to suggest consulting a local butcher, when the front doorbell rang. "Damn!" he swore as he rose to his feet. He threw a quick glance at Toni and seemed satisfied that she was amply covered from head to toe in the folds of his dark-green velour robe. He was dressed in jeans, dark socks, and a long-sleeved, unbuttoned shirt, the tail of which billowed out from his tanned body as he stalked from the room.

Toni added fresh coffee to her bright-blue mug, then sat back. Only hours ago her life had been uncertain and confusing, but now it stretched invitingly before her, made more wonderful and exciting by Christian's love.

Even the mind-boggling prospect of arranging their wedding in only a few days failed to cast the tiniest cloud of panic upon the warm glow surrounding her. It was the unexpected sound of voices raised in anger that finally penetrated her state of euphoria.

She looked toward the door just as an angry-faced Steven stepped into the room. He came to an abrupt halt, his disbelieving gaze riveted to Toni's robe-clad body and the tousled disarray of her dark hair.

Mr. Barr," she said with a contented sigh, her arms stealing around his neck. "But I do like to see a man put his whole heart into a project, don't you? I keep remembering something about 'practice makes perfect.' Do you get my drift?"

"Indeed, Miss Grant, indeed," Christian agreed. "I have three days in which to practice," he said huskily as he laid her on the bed, then began to remove his clothes. "Does that meet with your approval?"

"I approve of you." Toni smiled as she shrugged off the robe and then opened her arms to him. "Always and forever," she whispered as his large, tanned body covered hers and his strong arms swallowed her.

"I love you, Antonia," he rasped hoarsely as he took her.

"I love you, Christian," Toni whispered as magic surrounded them and ushered them upward to an exploding world of passion and desire.

with startled eyes as her former fiancé was gripped by one arm and swung completely around to face her future husband.

"You never learn, do you, Crowell?" Christian growled, his face contorted with anger. "Antonia will soon be my wife, and no one talks to her the way you've just done."

Toni saw Steven's free hand clench into a fist; she saw his arm begin an upward motion that would ultimately collide with Christian's jaw. But Christian was the faster of the two. She could hardly believe the speed with which he blocked the uppercut.

The next few seconds would always remain somewhat of a blur in Toni's mind. With the same quickness, Christian hustled Steven through the house and nearly threw him out the front door.

Several minutes passed before he returned to the kitchen and Toni, who was calmly clearing the table and placing the dirty dishes in the dishwasher.

She glanced up at him as he walked over and stood close beside her. "I'm sorry that you always seem to be fighting my battles," she said quietly.

"I'm not." Christian grinned. "As I told you last night, Antonia, life with you is so peaceful . . . so tranquil."

"I also remember telling you once that I wasn't sure you had the stamina to pursue me." She gave him a mischievous grin. "Are you still game?" she asked huskily.

"I thought I'd settled that point once and for all," he said calmly, then leaned down, swept her up into his arms, and walked into the bedroom. "Obviously I need to restate my claim."

"Oh, I understood the first effort on your behalf,

"Obviously you forgot I would be coming by this morning," he said in a tight, disapproving voice.

Oh, no! Toni thought wildly. *How on earth could I have forgotten about Steven?* But the answer was simple, she realized. Christian and the assurance of his love had wiped all else from her mind—especially Steven.

"I'm sorry, Steven," she said quietly. She pushed back her chair and stood, one hand going to the front of the robe and holding it together. "I . . . really . . ."

"At a loss for words, Toni?" Steven said with a sneer. "No wonder you didn't want me to follow you. You'd already decided to have a go at a bigger fish, hadn't you?"

Toni stared at him with dark eyes gone cold with anger. "The last time we had a similar confrontation, Steven, I distinctly remember you telling me I should ignore whatever embarrassment you might have caused me, and be thankful that I'd soon be your wife.

"Well . . ." She released her hold on the front of the robe in order to cross her arms over her chest, her palms cupping her elbows. "I suggest you take some of your own advice. Why don't you ignore whatever embarrassment you might have caused me by coming here today, and be thankful that I didn't take a horsewhip to your worthless hide the minute I set eyes on you!"

A dull red stain spread over Steven's face at her attack. "Still the same smart-mouthed little bitch, aren't you?" he snarled. "I wonder how long it will be before Barr tires of you and tosses you aside?"

Without warning, a raging Christian materialized in the doorway directly behind Steven. Toni watched